Once, twice…Julie's lashes fluttered open on the third try. "Why are we sitting here with the car idling?"

"We're waiting for the door to open."

"Well, it's not opening. The electronic beam must be…" Her voice trailed off as she exchanged a look with Billy. "There *is* no electronic beam, is there?"

"No, ma'am. We're slumming it. It's manually operated."

She climbed out of the car, then lifted the heavy aluminum garage door as if she had been doing it all her life. She whirled toward Billy and clapped enthusiastically for herself. "It was easier to deal with than the rotary phone," she called out. "I have great potential for becoming an ordinary woman."

"Not a chance, lady," Billy whispered, unable to take his eyes off her. Her magnificent eyes were flashing, and her lavish smile was enough to break a former undercover cop's heart.…

Dear Reader,

Welcome to the world of Silhouette Desire, where you can indulge yourself every month with romances that can only be described as passionate, powerful and provocative!

Popular author Cait London offers you *Gabriel's Gift,* this April's MAN OF THE MONTH. We're sure you'll love this tale of lovers once separated who reunite eighteen years later and must overcome the past before they can begin their future together.

The riveting Desire miniseries TEXAS CATTLEMAN'S CLUB: LONE STAR JEWELS continues with *Her Ardent Sheikh* by Kristi Gold, in which a dashing sheikh must protect a free-spirited American woman from danger.

In *Wife with Amnesia* by Metsy Hingle, the estranged husband of an amnesiac woman seeks to win back her love…and to save her from a mysterious assailant. Watch for Metsy Hingle's debut MIRA title, *The Wager,* in August 2001. Barbara McCauley's hero "wins" a woman in a poker game in *Reese's Wild Wager,* another tantalizing addition to her SECRETS! miniseries. Enjoy a contemporary "beauty and the beast" story with Amy J. Fetzer's *Taming the Beast.* And Ryanne Corey brings you a runaway heiress who takes a walk on the wild side with the bodyguard who's fallen head over heels for her in *The Heiress & the Bodyguard.*

Be sure to treat yourself this month, and read all six of these exhilarating Desire novels!

Enjoy!

Joan Marlow Golan

Joan Marlow Golan
Senior Editor, Silhouette Desire

Please address questions and book requests to:
Silhouette Reader Service
U.S.: 3010 Walden Ave., P.O. Box 1325, Buffalo, NY 14269
Canadian: P.O. Box 609, Fort Erie, Ont. L2A 5X3

The Heiress &
the Bodyguard

RYANNE COREY

Published by Silhouette Books
America's Publisher of Contemporary Romance

SILHOUETTE BOOKS

ISBN 0-373-76362-X

THE HEIRESS & THE BODYGUARD

Visit Silhouette at www.eHarlequin.com

Printed in U.S.A.

Books by Ryanne Corey

Silhouette Desire

The Valentine Street Hustle #615
Leather and Lace #657
The Stranger #764
When She Was Bad #950
Lady with a Past #1319
The Heiress & the Bodyguard #1362

RYANNE COREY

An author of bestselling romance novels, Ryanne Corey lives in Idaho in the shadow of the Teton Mountains, "the best place in the world to write and write and write." She has written over twenty novels and is recognized for the true-to-life humor and sensuality of her characters. She has received several awards over the past few years, including the *Romantic Times Magazine* Best Novel and Lifetime Achievement Awards. She has long believed that life is too serious to be taken too seriously. In her writing she enjoys creating appealing and amusing characters that take their first breath on page one, endearing themselves to the readers long after the book is finished. "For me," Ryanne says, "bringing a smile to someone's face is what life is all about."

Nothing is more satisfying to her than hearing from readers who share her enjoyment of "love and laughter." You can write to her at P.O. Box 328, Tetonia, ID 83452. Please include a SASE if a reply is desired.

One

This job was cake.

Billy Lucas lay stretched out on the bed, a banana Popsicle in his hand and three sinfully comfortable feather pillows behind his back. The Popsicle and the pillows were perks of the job. Ask for anything you need, Harris Roper had told him.

Being Billy, he'd taken advantage of the offer. Besides, there was a lovely Latin maid who hustled over from the kitchen whenever he ordered food. She spoke no English, but had beautiful black eyes and giggled whenever Billy winked at her. Whatever it took to draw a woman's attention, Billy had in spades. It was a gift he had enjoyed thoroughly in his life, but never abused. He respected women deeply, but had little regard for his own ability to make a lasting commitment. Life was far too interesting to settle down in the suburbs. Even the thought made him shiver.

His room had originally been intended for a chauffeur, or so he assumed. He had not been born into the Palm Beach set, but rather into the crime-ridden Oakland, California, set. They didn't have apartments for the chauffeur where he grew up. They had bars on the windows and jagged broken bottles topping cinder-block fences. The fine art of staying alive had kept him on his toes, however. Never once in his thirty-three years had he felt the boredom he'd seen on the faces of these poor Palm Beach trust-fund babies.

And he knew what he was talking about. There were five separate camera monitors mounted on the ceiling above his bed. One gave him a panoramic view of the front of the pink-tiled palace, another covered the walkway leading to the guesthouse. One covered the west side of the guesthouse, another the east side, which included the garage. And the last camera—his personal favorite— gave him a close-up of Julie Roper's front door.

For nearly two weeks now, he had watched Julie's comings and goings night and day. On the rare occasions when she went out alone, he was an invisible shadow. Once, very late at night, he'd followed her down to the beach, watching from the redwood dock as she'd skipped barefoot through the surf. She'd actually *skipped,* like a child who could hardly contain her own energy. He'd known then she was one lady he would never be able to predict, which made the job all the more interesting. She had pure class written all over her. Her shoulder-length hair was dark blond, artfully streaked with platinum, and whenever she walked, her shoulders were thrown back and her head held high. Billy had never seen an actual princess, but he imagined princesses would walk something like Julie Roper did. She dressed with the classy nonchalance of someone who could afford the best, but who put on the first thing in her closet and forgot about it. She was small, with fine bones and a look of fragility, which he was beginning to suspect might be deceptive. For whatever reason, she chose to live in the small guesthouse rather than the palatial main house. He was having a hard time getting a fix on her personality, which was very unusual for Billy Lucas. He was famous in his humble circles for being able to predict someone's next move with uncanny accuracy, but little Julie Roper kept him guessing. A gazillion-dollar heiress skipping through the surf? A woman who chose to live in a cottage rather than a palace? A woman who was terribly easy on the eyes, yet had no dates beyond an occasional evening with a stocky fellow who looked like a marine sergeant? No kisses, no cuddling, just a bear hug at her door.

And speak of the devil...

Billy perked up, watching as she emerged from the stucco monstrosity he had dubbed the Palm Beach Hilton. Her short white-sequined dress, slim-fitting but modest, sparkled as she strolled down the well-lit pathway to the guesthouse. She walked slowly, as if she had no place to go and all the time in the world to get there. Her head was down, her hair obscuring the expression on her face. Even her posture looked different, more brokenhearted than cool and composed. Her small figure looked incredibly defenseless, a little blond angel framed on either side by hedges of vibrant tropical blooms.

Something was wrong.

Change camera. She walked slowly to her front door, motion-sensitive lights keeping her well-illuminated. She punched in a security code beside the door, then disappeared inside. The windows of the cottage lit up one by one.

Shirtless, his longish dark hair tumbled, he sat up on

the edge of the bed. His heavy-lidded blue eyes took on a new intensity as he kept them on the camera. He might not be able to predict Julie Roper, but he knew when trouble was brewing. That talent had kept him alive and almost in one piece after working the gang unit in Oakland for eight years. Three puckered scars on his back from bullet wounds gave witness to his survival instinct. Another jagged scar on his abdomen above his low-riding jeans was a memento of his one and only stab wound. It was a sad fact, but most everyone on the streets, good guys and bad, had guns these days. His third trip to the hospital had resulted in a medal of valor and an early retirement from life as an undercover cop. He hadn't minded. He'd known for some time he was pushing his luck. Besides, he liked the idea of setting up a little security business for himself. There was very little chance of being shot while baby-sitting the rich and the paranoid.

Billy watched Julie's shadow crossing back and forth behind the blinds of the bedroom window. Suddenly, she was moving quickly, as if now she had a purpose. Billy shrugged on a flowered shirt and started putting on his runners, never taking his eye off the cameras for more than a few seconds at a time. *What are you doing, little sister?*

And then he had his answer. The garage door opened, spilling a square of light on the driveway. Billy stood up and grabbed for his wallet, watching as Julie's Porsche backed out at thirty miles an hour, tires squealing. The lady was in a hurry. This was no midnight visit to the beach.

Billy knew his Rent-a-Wreck would have a tough time keeping up with the Porsche, particularly with an emotional blonde driving the fancy car. He grabbed his cell phone and sprinted out of the apartment like a bat out of hell, with no time to obey Harris Roper's number-one rule of little sister surveillance: Call me immediately if anything unusual happens.

Billy could take the time to call Harris and risk losing his charge, or follow Julie and call Harris ASAP.

Some decisions practically made themselves.

For Julie, it had started out as an ordinary, yawn-stifling evening. Harris had thrown one of his exclusive parties, inviting the few acquaintances he deemed suitable to associate with his sister. Her brother had terribly high standards, and none of his friends were particularly outgoing. Still, they could all trace their ancestry back to the *Mayflower,* and each and every one was on the Forbes 500 list of wealthiest people. As usual, the party had turned out to be very small and very subdued. The ladies congregated on the sofa, keeping their legs crossed and their hands folded modestly in their laps. The gentlemen were gathered at the mirror-backed bar, drinking little but gazing often at the splendid figures they made in their designer tuxedos. The one exception to this was Beauregard James Farquhar III, a Palm Beach trust-fund baby who sat next to Julie, stood next to Julie and walked beside Julie the entire evening. He was a long-time friend of the family, a man Harris deeply respected for his financial acumen, impeccable manners and doggedly patient character. He looked like a tennis pro, with tanned skin, a perfectly trimmed blond crew cut and a square face that always reminded Julie of a young Ted Kennedy. Beau had returned from a wine-and-spirits tour of Europe that very day, a good ten pounds heavier than when last she'd seen him. He'd proclaimed himself "frightfully happy" to see Julie; indeed, he had been frightfully happy to see her on each and every occasion since Julie could remember. He was completely devoted to her and had been since she was eighteen. She had managed to keep him at arm's length until she returned home from college a few months earlier. Prior to his leaving for Europe, he'd been constantly underfoot, rather like a co-dependent housepet. Julie knew it was only a matter of time before Beau asked her to marry him. Her twenty-third birthday was hanging on the horizon like a dreadful storm cloud. Beau had hinted that this year her special day would be truly a monumental occasion. He had also asked her ring size. Julie had suffered from a nasty case of hives ever since.

Although it was not yet 10:00 p.m., Julie was wrestling with an overriding urge to take a nap in the middle of Harris's party. The pianist her brother had hired for the evening was like a musical sandman, playing "Somewhere over the Rainbow" ever so softly. She sat on the sofa next to Beau and tried to appear interested in his detailed description of a smooth yet complex little cabernet he'd discovered in Italy. Unfortunately, Beau knew his wines, and could go on forever rhapsodizing about the subtle integration of aromatics and tannins. Julie had fallen asleep twice, her lolling head connecting painfully with the carved sofaback. Finally she'd pleaded a headache and politely excused herself from the festivities.

The urge to sleep left her the moment she walked into the small guesthouse she called home. Away from Beau, the pianist and all talk of financial dealings, she was suddenly wide-awake and positively smoking with restlessness. She decided to take her Porsche out for a spin before bed. She didn't bother changing from her evening dress, although she did lose the panty hose and exchange her high heels for a comfortable pair of high-top sneakers. She looked utterly ridiculous but felt more comfortable than she had all evening. Besides, no one would see her. More than likely, Harris wouldn't even know she had left the grounds.

She drove mindlessly, enjoying the cool air on her flushed cheeks and pondering the strange culture of the well-bred and confused. She'd mingled with Palm Beach's finest families sporadically throughout her life, yet she always felt like a stranger in their midst. Six months earlier, she had graduated from a private women's college, and now poor Harris didn't know what to do with her. The two jobs she'd had since then had lasted four weeks and four days, respectively. First, she'd given in to Harris and accepted a job on the board of Roper Industries, doing what seemed to her absolutely nothing for an obscene amount of money. She had traveled to work with Harris, had lunch with Harris and traveled home with Harris. By week four she was bored to tears and told Harris she thought her destiny lay elsewhere. On her own, she had found a job as a personal shopper at a terribly chic oceanside boutique. It wasn't something she wanted to make a career of, but she thought it might keep her occupied while she tried to figure out what to do with the rest of her life. Unfortunately, the self-absorbed clientele, set hours and lack of challenge was worse than working at Roper Industries. She was "voluntarily unemployed" after only four days. Harris was becoming more and more concerned about her future, and he made no secret of that fact. He was a dear soul, but a chronic, intense, agonizing worrier. Julie had been seven years old and Harris only twenty-one when their parents had been killed in a sailing accident. Julie thought of them often, remembering sparkling, beautiful people full of love, laughter and spontaneity. She had no idea how two such oddball personalities as Harris and herself had emerged from the family gene pool. Harris had done his best for her through the past sixteen years, but his responsibilities had been terribly heavy for one so young. He obsessed over her welfare as he obsessed over the management of the family fortune. Julie hadn't realized just how much it had all worn on him until she'd returned from college. Suddenly he looked far older than his thirty-seven years, with shadow-rimmed blue eyes, pale skin and shoulders that hinted at weariness. Julie had tried to make him understand she wasn't his responsibility any longer, but Harris continued to worry himself to death when it came to her safety and security. The Roper mansion might have some forty-odd rooms, but Julie was plagued with overwhelming claustrophobia. Harris was here, there and everywhere, forever anxious and apprehensive. It had taken Julie months to talk him into allowing her to move from the main house to the guesthouse. Two weeks earlier he had positively stunned her by finally giving his permission. This had given her hope that someday she would be able to actually move off the grounds...until Beau had made it clear it was only a matter of days until he popped the big question. Julie had listened with barely disguised horror, visualizing a helium balloon going *boom*.

Seeking advice on the best way to let Beau down, she'd approached Harris on the subject. His reaction had been uncharacteristically vehement. Although he didn't go so far as to actually raise his voice, he demanded to know how long Julie was going to skim the surface of life like a paranoid butterfly, never committing to anything or anyone. She couldn't do any better than Beau, and he had certainly proven himself to be truly devoted. She had to dedicate herself to *something* someday. Why not now? Why not a fine, decent fellow like Beau?

Why not indeed? Julie thought. Beau certainly wasn't the man she dreamed of, but the faceless fantasy she had visualized probably didn't exist. Each night in her dreams her imagination went for a walk and came back with a mysterious, thrilling superhero who inspired a great deal more than respect. Logically, however, she knew Beau Farquhar would never mistreat her, and he'd proven long ago he was hopelessly devoted. The man was steady, persistent, kind, persistent, good-natured and persistent. He was also persistent. Why not indeed? Poor Harris had worried himself sick over her welfare too long as it was. She wasn't particularly interested in getting married nor was she particularly determined to stay single. Quite honestly, she wasn't particularly focused on anything. The death of her parents at such an impressionable age had left Julie emotionally scarred, wary of attachments which could result in vulnerability. Harris had been the only constant in her world. She loved her brother deeply and would do almost anything to repay him for all the sacrifices he had made on her behalf. She had been his responsibility for far too long.

And so it came down to this: realistically, she knew there was very little chance of her falling head over heels in love. She truly believed it was an impossibility, given her own fear of caring too deeply for anyone or anything. Beau was a good man who knew her well and expected very little. Harris obviously thought the match was made in heaven. If he thought it was the best thing for her, it probably was. Heaven knew Harris deserved a life of his own. He would never concentrate on his own happiness until Julie's welfare was secured.

She continued driving for well over an hour. She didn't care where she was going, she only knew she had to be someplace else. Eventually she lost the lights of the city, finding herself on a narrow two-lane road crowded on both sides with thick cypress. It was too dark to see anything beyond the shadows of foliage surrounding her. The air grew heavy and wet, as if she were heading into a swamp. She'd never been in an actual swamp before, but the word *alligator* kept popping into her mind. She was terrified of animals whose teeth were larger than her own. Her palms on the steering wheel became wet.

Julie wasn't accustomed to checking the gas gauge in her car. In fact, all the maintenance on the Porsche was done by Harris's "people," invisible and ever-diligent. Usually Harris insisted she used his car and driver if she needed to go out. When she did drive her own car, it was always ready, bright and shiny and filled with gas. Naturally she knew such things as oil and fuel were necessary for a car to run, but the particulars of it all had never been a concern.

Until the Porsche sputtered, coughed and died. The gas gauge read empty.

She managed to pull over to the side of the road before the car came to a complete stop. Greenery scratched eerily against the passenger window, sounding like someone trying to get in. She panicked, locking the doors and putting on her seat belt for the first time, as if this would save her from her predicament. Other words scuttled through her mind besides *alligator: snakes, spiders, green slimy things.* Beyond the windshield, the circles of the headlights barely illuminated ten feet of the utter void surrounding her. In her conscious mind she knew it wasn't a good idea to leave the lights on when the engine wasn't running. She also knew there was no way in heaven or hell she was going to sit in utter darkness. She turned on the interior light and tried to find the emergency flasher lights, but nothing she punched, pulled or turned did a thing, beyond turning the windshield wipers on. She asked herself what a true heroine would do in this situation. She answered herself: she probably would have had the sense to put gas in the car in the first place. Still, she could simply call Harris on the cell phone...if she'd had the foresight to bring the phone with her. Her beautifully manicured nails tapped a frantic rhythm on the steering wheel. What to do, what to do...?

From out of nowhere, a car pulled up beside her and stopped. The driver sat in shadows, but she had the impression of a portly build and a bushy beard. He motioned for her to roll down her window. Julie shook her head frantically. He held up two hands as if saying, *How do you expect me to help you, then?*

They'll find my body dumped by the roadside, she thought despairingly. Not right away, but in a few days when the humidity and heat and alligators have taken their toll. She would look utterly terrible for the funeral. Poor Harris would think it was all his fault for allowing her to live in the guesthouse and be guilt-ridden the rest of his life. And he would never have an answer to the million-dollar question: What on earth was Julie thinking, driving through *that* sort of neighborhood?

Suddenly a hand tapping on her window interrupted her morbid musings. She jumped as high as her seat belt would allow her, staring into dark eyes that looked glazed and unfocused. He looked about forty years old, a very large man with more hair on his arms and face than his head. He wore a thin white undershirt stained on the front in several places.

Her panic doubled and redoubled in the space of five seconds. She might not have much experience with men, but she knew this person walking around in his underwear was not the answer to her prayers.

"Do you need help?" he shouted.

Julie shook her head frantically.

"Can I give you a ride?"

Julie shook her head harder, her brown eyes enormous.

At this point he dropped his smile and tried to open the driver's-side door. If Julie had been able to breathe, she would have screamed. Unfortunately, the only sound she could make was short and faint, like a baby hiccup. For whatever reason, she pressed her hand on the horn and kept it there.

It took a moment before she realized another car had pulled up directly behind her. She wondered what the possibilities were of two men with extremely bad intentions happening upon her in this tropical wilderness. Was there a convention of highway muggers somewhere near here? Did these sort of people lie waiting in the dark for idiots like herself to run out of gas?

At that point, everything happened quickly, like a nightmare in fast-forward. The driver of the second car got out, leaving his engine running and the lights on. He said something to white-undershirt person, but Julie still had her hand on the horn so she couldn't hear. There was the briefest scuffle outside her window; she saw the whirl of a flowered shirt and a fist flying. Almost immediately the fellow who'd been trying to get inside her car dropped out of sight.

Two arms leaned against her door. Her rescuer—at least she hoped he was her rescuer—leaned down to look inside. He had longish dark hair that covered his ears, moving softly around his face with the night wind. She couldn't make out the color of his eyes, but saw them sparkle, as if he were greatly amused.

"Stop that," he mouthed, pointing at her hand on the horn, then at his own ears.

For whatever reason, Julie did as she was told. She

continued to stare at him like a helpless deer caught in the headlights.

"Thank you," he said when the noise suddenly stopped. He grinned at her, showing very white teeth against a very tan face. For a simple smile, it was amazingly powerful, glinting in his eyes, denting his cheeks and lending an aura of boyish charm to very masculine features. Julie was reassured enough to roll down her window one-half inch.

"Looks like you've got yourself in a sticky situation," he said.

Julie cocked her head, trying to see where the worrisome bearded person had gone to. "Did you *kill* him?" she asked, her voice trembling with nerves.

He looked perplexed. "Why on earth would I kill him? You're a complete stranger. Don't take offense, but I really don't want to go to jail for someone I don't even know."

"Did you beat him *unconscious?*" she persisted, warming to her subject.

He rolled his eyes. "Has anyone ever told you that you're a little dramatic? He told me if I knew what was good for me, I'd keep driving. I told him I'd never done what was good for me and hit him once. Now he's taking a nap here on the road. He'll be fine." He paused, added, "Except for the black eye he'll have. So what are you doing out here in the wee hours of the morning? If you don't mind my asking."

The window went down another inch. "I'm sitting here because my car broke."

"What do you mean, it broke?"

"It's out of gas."

He considered this for a moment, and the grin came

back. "Yeah, I guess that would break it all right. So how can I help?"

"Well…" Julie considered her options, starting up the tapping on the steering wheel again. "Do you happen to know where I am?"

He bit his lip, trying not to laugh out loud. "You're a couple of hours north of the coast." He paused. "The Florida coast."

"I know I'm in Florida," Julie replied indignantly. "I just wondered if there was a town nearby, somewhere I could get some gas."

"I'm a tourist, so I'm afraid I don't know. I'm exploring myself. I'd be happy to give you a lift to a gas station, if you'd like."

"That's probably not a good idea," she said nervously. "I should be able to handle this myself." Still, there was such an enormous difference between *should* and *could*.

"Whatever," he shrugged. "This isn't exactly a freeway, so you may be here for a while. Keep your doors locked, especially when what's-his-name here wakes up. He won't be a happy camper. See ya."

"Hold it!" Julie's yelp stopped him from walking away. She rolled her window down another two inches. "Maybe I will take you up on your offer, if I won't be putting you out."

"Fine by me." He lifted his hand, sticking four fingers through the top of the window. "I'm Billy."

"Julie," she said, taking his lead and foregoing last names. Hesitantly she took the tips of his fingers in her hand and shook them politely. "How do you do?"

This time Billy laughed, the sound rich and deep, lingering in the heavy air. "How do *you* do? Has anyone ever told you that you look a lot like Grace Kelly? Same voice, too. Very cultured."

"Is that good?"

"If you like Grace Kelly. I loved her myself." He stepped back, hooking his thumbs into the pockets of his jeans. "I don't want to scare you, but you'll need to get out of your car if this is going to work."

Julie still hesitated. "Maybe I should sit here and wait for you to bring some gas back."

Billy sighed, digging his wallet from the back pocket of his jeans. He flipped it open, allowing her to see the flash of his old police badge. As a retired cop, this was highly illegal. That fact didn't stop Billy from doing it now and again. "You couldn't be safer, ma'am. I'm an officer of the law, sworn to protect and serve the citizens of California when I'm not on vacation. I wouldn't do anything mean to the citizens of Florida, either. Could we hurry this up? The mosquitoes are eating me alive."

Julie realized this was the first time she had met an actual public policeman. The well-dressed private security people Harris hired were nice, but hardly battle-scarred veterans of the streets. Immediately her mind took off on a fantasy flight, imagining the dire and dangerous situations he must face in his work. How thrilling. "Do you shoot people?"

He assumed a terribly serious expression. "Only very bad people who shoot at me first."

"Where do you keep your gun?"

Billy almost lost it at that point. He stared down at the toes of his runners for a good fifteen seconds before he could talk. "I'm on vacation," he finally managed. "Besides, the shoulder holster would look terrible with this shirt. Any more questions?"

"Not at the moment," Julie said graciously, turning off the interior light and pushing the button to unlock the car doors. "I *do* appreciate your help."

"Hold it a minute," Billy told her. If she got out now, she would step on the beer belly of her unconscious, not-so-good Samaritan. He took him by the arms and pulled him away from the Porsche. "Okay, princess. Your carriage awaits."

Princess, Julie thought, smiling to herself. This was getting better and better. She couldn't have come up with a more perfect hero if she'd tried. He was an authority figure, an officer of the law. He had gone into battle for her. He was charming. He was absolutely *gorgeous.* Her nervous tension was gradually being replaced by unexpected excitement.

She got out of the car, sparing a quick look at the fellow in the undershirt. He appeared to be sleeping peacefully. "Are you going to report this?" she asked Billy.

"As soon as I can," he replied, thinking of poor Harris Roper. While following Julie, he'd tried using the cell phone, only to realize the battery was out of juice. He'd have to do this the old-fashioned way and use a pay phone as soon as he could. "It's part of the job, princess."

Two

___

Up close and personal, little Julie Roper packed a wallop. From the top of her designer gown to the toes of her absurd sneakers, she was clearly one-of-a kind.

She wasn't cool, self-centered or spoiled, the way Billy had imagined a heiress would be. She was nervous, but Billy sensed the nervousness was something she was enjoying. She talked like someone had put a quarter in her, asking him questions at the speed of light.

Do you like your job?

Do you enjoy danger?

Have you ever been shot?

What do you mean, *a few times?*

Twisting sideways in her seat, blond hair flying every which way from the open window, she demanded every detail. Billy shook his head, assuming a deeply troubled expression. "I can't really talk about it. It brings back such horrible memories." Which, of course, was another bit of fiction. In reality he was rather proud of his war wounds, keeping all three bullets surgeons had dug out of him in a peanut-butter jar in his closet. Still, he was beginning to sense Julie Roper would be impossible to send home like a good little girl if she enjoyed her adventure any more than she seemed to be doing already.

"I'm terribly sorry," Julie said earnestly. "Truly, I didn't mean to open any old wounds—" She stopped, realizing what she'd said. "Gracious. I didn't mean that the way it sounded. Oh, dear."

"No problem," Billy muttered. It wasn't often he found himself in a situation that made him uncomfortable, but Julie Roper did just that. She was a bundle of brown-eyed enthusiasm, using her hands as she talked, her animated face illuminated in the yellow light from the dashboard. There was no artifice about her, nothing pretentious. This was the woman-child he had seen skipping in the surf. This was the true Julie Roper. Part child, part woman and apparently starving for a taste of life with all its adventures and dangers.

In all his experience, he'd never come across a woman quite like her. He began to worry.

"Is there someone at home you should be calling?" he asked abruptly. "Someone who might be terribly worried about you? Someone you need to get home to?"

Julie shook her head, absently tucking her hair behind her ears. "Not really. I left him a note just in case. I said I needed to get away for a couple of hours, and not to worry."

"Husband?" Billy asked, since it was the logical response.

"No. My brother Harris. It's just the two of us."

"Then he'll probably be going crazy when he realizes you're gone," Billy said, trying to implant a seed of guilt.

"I don't want to pry, but...when exactly did you leave home?"

Julie shrugged. "I don't know. Two, three hours ago."

"And within that time, you've run out of gas, been accosted by a drunk, and been forced to accept a ride from a total stranger. Kind of a bad track record, don't you think?"

"I accepted a ride from you," she pointed out defensively, "because you are a policeman."

"Whatever," Billy replied, shoving a frustrated hand through his long black hair. "My point is, if all this can happen to you in three or four hours, what could happen to you in a few days? This is just a guess, but...you don't run off by yourself very often, right?"

"I could do it every week, for all you know."

"If you did it every week, you would remember to check the gas gauge in your car. You would also know where you are, not to mention where you are going."

Julie considered this for a moment, her lips pinched tight. "I don't care for the way you put that, but you're right. This was kind of a spur-of-the-moment thing, if you know what I mean. Still, it's turning out better than I hoped."

Billy slanted her an incredulous look. "Are you kidding?"

"Well, I met you," she said, her eyes shining like copper pennies and a high flush of color on her cheekbones. "You are by far the most interesting person I have ever met in my life."

Billy could barely stop himself from groaning out loud. "You must not get out much, then. Which, by the way, is probably going to be the reason your brother is going to worry about you. Are the two of you close?"

"Yes," Julie said, "and no. We love each other, but

neither one of us is exactly…comfortable…with our lives right now. Harris has been the father figure for a long time, and it's wearing on him. I just do as I'm told so the poor man doesn't worry any more than necessary.''

''You do as you're told? Well, that explains everything. Your brother must have told you to drive around Florida in the middle of the night.''

''Very funny. It's not a crime to take a little ride.''

''I doubt he'll see it that way.''

''How could you possibly know that? You don't know the situation, you've just met me and you don't know Harris at all. How could you possibly have any opinion on this?''

Billy found himself grinding his teeth. The little lady was not cooperating. He wasn't used to women who didn't cooperate with him, and the experience was a little frustrating. ''I'm not trying to pick a fight with you. I just know when someone is in over their head, that's all. You need to go home and rethink this thing.''

''My head,'' Julie retorted, ''is well above the water-line, so don't worry. For heaven's sake, you're as bad as Harris.''

I'm nothing like your brother, Billy wanted to throw back. *I know him, and I know you far better than you think.* Instead he contented himself with, ''I'm a man, and I know how men protect the people they love. I've had a little more experience with life than you have.'' Now there was the understatement of the year.

''That's exactly why I'm so glad we met,'' Julie exclaimed, putting her hand on his arm. ''You came along at such an opportune moment. I was feeling a little down tonight, because my birthday is coming and I'm going to…well, that's neither here nor there. At any rate, you actually *fought* someone on my behalf. I'll never forget this. Every now and then it's kind of a relief to just…just fly by the seat of your skirt.''

''Pants,'' Billy snapped, irritated by the way his body was reacting to her innocent touch. ''Fly by the seat of your *pants*. And don't romanticize this thing. I didn't fight with anyone on your behalf, I just pushed a drunk over sideways with one hand. I should have let him have a few more minutes with you. Then maybe you'd want to go home where you belong.''

''You're talking like a bodyguard or something.'' Miffed, Julie withdrew her hand, folding her arms across her chest. ''You should meet my brother. I'm sure the two of you would be the best of friends.''

Billy opened his mouth to tell her he was nothing like her damn brother, then put a choke-hold on the words. ''Whatever.''

''You say that a lot.''

''What?''

''Whatever. And you say it kind of like you're growling, like this—'*Whatever.*'''

Billy looked at the face she was pulling, at the way she wrinkled her nose and drew her eyebrows together fiercely. She was completely unselfconscious, oblivious to the disarming expression on her face, doing her very best to imitate a growl. A little blond pit bull in this instance, just another side of her personality to add to the fascinating repertoire.

He couldn't help himself. He turned his attention back to the road, smiling just a little. No, this was bad…he couldn't afford to lose his perspective. Never mix business with pleasure…or anything else, for that matter. She was business. Business, business, business.

His smile grew to an irrepressible grin, despite the lecture he was delivering to himself. He allowed himself a quick look, his eyes following the line of her cheekbone, the soft curves of her parted mouth. She had no idea he was staring. She had no idea how her hair drank in light, didn't realize how lush and ripe her baby-bowed mouth seemed to him. She even smelled like an unfamiliar delicacy, the fragrance subtle, lingering in the close confines of the car like music. Billy's blood was zinging through his veins like 98-proof adrenalin.

"Of all the damn things," he said softly, staring straight ahead.

"What?" she asked innocently, pulling her attention from the butterball moon hanging in the sky straight in front of them.

"Nothing."

Julie sighed, dropping her head back on the seat. "First it was *whatever*, now it's *nothing*. Has anyone ever told you that you're not particularly good at communicating your feelings?"

"Actually, no. Usually I'm quite good at communicating my…feelings. At least that's what I've been told."

"I expect you're not talking about verbal communication."

"I expect I'm not."

Julie closed her eyes, fighting a sudden and overwhelming fatigue. She wasn't used to all this excitement. Her petite figure looked incredibly defenseless against the unrelenting darkness of the window beyond. "I think…" She yawned, covering her mouth as if a lady should. "I think you're probably…sorry…you're stuck with me…"

He waited, and when she didn't continue, he realized she had fallen asleep. Just like that; one minute she was chattering like a trained parrot, the next she was sleeping like an angel. He allowed himself a longer look this time, fascinated for some strange reason by the way her hair looked caressing the long line of her throat.

"I expect I'm not sorry," he whispered.

She awoke to music—loud, thumping, migraine-promoting music.

"There's a nasty wake-up call," Billy said, amused.

Blinking her eyes, she looked around, realizing they were at a truck stop. Billy had pulled up to a gas pump, and on the other side of the pump, a low-rider Toyota truck jumped and rocked with deafening noise. Underneath the truck, fluorescent purple lights glowed brightly.

"Have I been asleep long?" she mumbled, sitting up and stretching her arms. "Where are we?"

"You were asleep about an hour," Billy said, turning off the engine. "And I haven't the faintest idea where we are. We're just lucky we stumbled across a gas station that's open in the middle of the night. This Rent-a-Wreck was about dry." Since he didn't want Julie to know he had a cell phone in the glove box, he was relieved to see a pay phone inside the small convenience store. He was itching to call Harris and assure the poor guy his sister was safe. "Look, I have to visit the rest room. Why don't you fill up the car while I'm gone? I'll borrow a gas can while I'm inside."

He was gone before she had time to form the words: *I've never filled up a car before.*

Which was probably good, Julie reasoned. Billy was already under the impression she was a mindless idiot; there was no reason to add fuel to that particular fire by confirming it.

All she had to do was add fuel to the car. And how hard could that be?

She got out of the car, wincing as the music from the

Toyota hit her full-force. It wasn't Chopin, but it was all part of the experience. She watched intently as a whip-cord-lean teenager jumped out of the truck, opened the little door to the gas tank and stuck the nozzle inside. Voilà.

The teenager looked over at her, his clean-shaven head glinting like a cue ball beneath the overhead lighting. "Hey," he said.

"Hey what?" she asked curiously, fiddling with the door to the gas tank.

He grinned. "Just hey, Blondie. Are you having a little trouble there?"

The little door wouldn't open. "No," she muttered, pulling at it with both hands. "It's just…stuck a little, I think."

He sauntered over, bringing a heavy aroma of cigarette smoke with him. "You can't open it from out here, or everyone would be siphoning your gas. Pop the safety latch inside."

She bit her lip, trying to translate this into Palm Beach language. "Pop what?"

"You're kidding, right? The door to the gas tank. Hell, haven't you ever filled up a car before?"

"Not this particular car," Julie said honestly. Nor any other car, but that was none of his business. "Could you show me where to…pop it?"

"I'd show you anything you want." He looped his skinny arm around her shoulders, guiding her over to the driver's side of the car. "You open the car door—like this—and pull that little lever—like this—and it pops the door to the gas tank open. Now pay attention and I'll demonstrate." He guided her back to the pump. "Pull the hose out. Twist the cap on the tank, put the hose in and push Start. See? It's that easy. What's your name?"

Julie was watching the gas pump intently, afraid the thing was going to overflow. "My what? Oh...Julie. Thank you for your help."

"I'm Jeff."

"Goodbye, Jeff."

"What's a pink and fluffy thing like you doing out here at 2:00 a.m.?"

"Is this thing going to stop on its own?"

He chuckled. "Poor baby. Whoever let you out alone after dark made a big mistake. Yeah, it will stop." His fingers kneaded her shoulder. "You owe me something, don't you think? Have you got a phone number?"

"Everyone has a phone number," Julie said irritably, twisting away from him.

"What are the chances you'd give it to me?"

"The chances of my adopting you would be greater," she said, tossing her hair back and staring him down as she would a fly, moth or any other insect annoying her. "Goodbye, Jeff."

"Not interested, huh?"

"No," Julie said with an overdose of sincerity, "but I'm sure I'll have wonderful memories about you for the rest of my life."

He held up both hands in surrender. "Your loss, Blondie."

"Let's talk about loss," Billy said.

Julie hadn't seen him approach, as most of her focus had been on the mysterious gas pump and the worrisome gurgling noises it was making. He was carrying a dented old gas can, which he put down directly in front of Jeff. "There are all kinds of loss," Billy went on, with a smile that didn't even begin to reach his eyes. "You can loose teeth, for one thing. That kind of loss is really painful. You don't want to lose any of your teeth, do you, kid?"

There was something about Billy's expression that made Julie plant herself between the two. "This isn't necessary. He was showing me how to make the gas pump work."

"*What*-ever," Billy replied, in his best growling fashion.

"Hey man, she needed help," the teenager said, quickly backing up as he talked. "She couldn't figure out how to fill the car up, so I helped her. Ask, if you don't believe me."

Billy raised one eyebrow at Julie. She nodded and he seemed to relax almost imperceptibly. "Okay, kid. You can leave."

Jeff didn't need a second invitation. The fluorescent laces on his combat boots flashed as he sprinted inside the truck stop to pay for his gas. Billy never took his eyes off Julie, not for a second. A muscle in his jaw was working hard and fast. "You really don't know how to fill up a car, do you?"

"If I did, would I embarrass myself like this?" Julie threw back, cheeks flaming. "He was just a baby, you didn't need to scare him. You were a baby once...or were you?"

"Never," Billy snapped. He was so frustrated, he wanted to kick something. Harris had just answered his private line when Billy had looked outside and seen Julie in what appeared to be yet another sticky situation. He'd hung up on the man to come to her rescue. "What is it with you? Didn't you learn the first time? Don't talk to strangers!"

"I never talk to strangers! I don't *know* any strangers!"

Billy thumped his head with the heel of his hand. "Why do I expect logic from you? Julie, that kid was a *stranger*. That drunk trying to get in your car was a *stranger.* Hell, *I'm* a stranger! You shouldn't be talking to any of us, don't you get that?''

"You're a policeman," Julie sniffed. "You're perfectly safe."

"What if I'm a *bad* policeman? Have you thought of that? You can't go around trusting everyone you meet, or you'll never get home. Learn from your mistakes."

At that point, Julie knew she was either going to cry or slap him. Before she could lift her hand, the tears were welling up in her soft brown eyes. "You don't need to talk to me like this," she sniffed. "I have enough on my mind without taking your abuse. You're overreacting, anyway. I'm not your responsibility. I know I'm not…familiar with some things, but I'm not stupid, either. Just take me back to my car and you can go on your merry way."

"And you'll go home?" Billy persisted, steeling himself against the weeping Bambi look.

"When I darn well please," Julie tossed back, refusing to be intimidated as easily as poor Jeff had been. "Which could be *months* from now!"

Silently, Billy counted to ten. Then, quite softly he said, "Get in the car. Now."

"And if I don't?" some devil made her say.

He took two steps, bringing his body three inches from hers. He dipped his head, letting the words swirl over her parted lips. "Then I'll spank the living daylights out of you, right here and right now."

"You wouldn't."

"*Ha!* Honey, at this point there's no telling what I'll do."

Brown eyes warred with blue for a good ten seconds. Julie gulped, lifted her chin and tried to say something to break the standoff, but the small movement closed the distance between them. For the space of a heartbeat she felt the touch of his lips on hers, no deeper than moonlight. Her body prickled fiercely like awakening flesh from top to bottom. And somewhere in the depths of her unconsciousness, she thought to herself, *I want more. Whatever this is, I want more.*

And so it was Billy who finally jumped back, Billy who threw open her car door and pushed her inside with barely restrained force. He'd known precisely what she was thinking, not only because she was too inexperienced to hide it, but because he was thinking the same thing.

More.

He decided he wasn't getting paid nearly enough for this job.

On the positive side, the not-so-good Samaritan was gone when they returned to the cypress jungle where Julie had abandoned her car. On the negative side, so was Julie's Porsche.

"Oh, my sainted aunt," she whispered, her jaw dropping. "Did I…could I have…I was so distracted, I may have left my keys—"

"—in the Porsche," Billy said in a flat voice. If he were an emotional man, he would seriously consider shedding a few tears at this point. He couldn't think of a time when he'd been so damned exasperated. "This is a real red-letter day for you, isn't it? In case no one has told you this, people who drive exotic sports cars are not supposed to leave the keys in the ignition."

"I'm not some kind of dimwit. Whether you believe it or not, I don't make a habit of leaving my keys in the ignition. I wasn't thinking straight at the time. That disgusting person who apparently made off with my car really had me rattled." She paused, blinking away the moisture gathering in her eyes. "What else could go wrong tonight?"

Despite his own frustration, Billy wanted to erase the forlorn look on her beautiful face. "Look at the bright side, kiddo. He left you that fine 1969 Ford pickup for trade. You could sell it for parts."

A loud sniff. "These kinds of things never happened before."

"Welcome to the real world. So what now?"

Julie looked at Billy sideways, biting her lip. "Well…I might need another little ride."

"Another little ride?"

"Just to a telephone," she assured him. "We could head back in the general direction of Palm Beach and stop at the first telephone we come across. I'll just call Harris and…you could go on your merry way."

Billy's forehead thumped on the steering wheel. "I feel like I'm in a nightmare and can't wake up," he muttered. "You're like a little tornado, creating havoc wherever you touch down. I really feel for your poor brother."

"My poor brother won't know I'm gone until the morning." Julie's lower lip quivered ever so slightly. "And there's no need to be insulting. We all have our areas of expertise."

Despite everything, Billy's mouth tipped up on one side. "That's true. I was under the impression you're in the habit of depending on others, but maybe I was mistaken. Tell me, your area of expertise would be…?"

Julie thought. What on earth was she supposed to say, *I'm a pro at using a charge card?* "My area of expertise is none of your business. Suffice it to say I have one. Several. I have *several* areas of expertise."

He smiled, his mouth curved with a hint of tenderness. He was finding it terribly hard to stay angry with her.

He'd thought he had seen everything in his gritty days as an undercover cop, but he'd never come across a woman with so much spirit and so little experience to back it up. Strangely enough, he almost envied her in a wistful sort of way. What would it be like to have so little experience with the world that you expected the best from everyone? The way Billy figured it, if you had no illusions or expectations, they weren't going to blow up in your face. Though it had never been a conscious choice he'd made, he'd been disillusioned almost from day one. When Billy was two years old, his father had gone out one night for a beer and never come back. His mother had her hands full keeping them both fed and clothed while she worked her way through school to get her RN degree. She'd done her best, but she didn't have the time or resources to protect him from reality. Five years after she'd achieved her dream and become a nurse, she was diagnosed with leukemia. She had died four agonizing months later, with Billy by her side. The last thing she had said to him was "I'm sorry." He had the feeling she wasn't apologizing for dying on him, but for the circumstances under which she'd brought him into the world.

At that point, Billy began charting his own course. He'd decided early on to look at life as a very dangerous game. The more dangerous you were, the more likely you were to stay alive. He always expected the worst from his adversaries and was seldom disappointed. In Billy's world, innocence was a weakness. Purity was extinct and idealism was a terrible flaw. It could get you killed.

This world was *not* a pretty place, damn it. Why did spending a couple of hours with Julie Roper make him wonder if he might have missed a rainbow somewhere along the way? He told himself he was an idiot, yet continued to watch her, devouring her with his thoughts. She dropped into the passenger seat of his car and slammed the door with a frustrated sigh.

"All I wanted was to go on a drive," she whispered. "No Harris, no Beau, no chauffeur—"

"Wait a second. Who's Beau?"

"What? Oh…he's a friend. I just wanted some time to myself, no one escorting me, no one waiting anxiously for me to come back. Just a ride, that's all I wanted."

Just a ride, she'd said, but Billy heard the tremor of loneliness and defeat in her voice. With an odd sense of surprise, he realized he had been wrong about her motives. This wasn't a joyride or even a small rebellion against a spoiled and privileged existence. This was something quite different. He watched the moistness gather in her eyes, saw the glitter of a single tear rolling down her soft cheek.

Billy was no stranger to a woman's tears, but more often than not, they came from the wives, mothers or girlfriends of someone he'd locked up. Like everyone else in his line of work, he'd been trained to offer a professional compassion, which stopped short of genuine sympathy. As a matter of fact, he'd been famous for his emotional detachment.

Cool, calm and controlled under any circumstances. Yes, siree.

"Will you please not do that?" he said abruptly, an unusual tightness in his throat.

Julie sniffed loudly. "Do what?"

"That *thing* you keep doing. Crying." Billy searched his pockets, coming up with a napkin from a fast-food joint. He was lucky to find that. He was the sort of man who carried a gun, not a nice white handkerchief. "Here. Blow your nose, and…and think happy thoughts." Hell, he sounded like Mary Poppins.

Julie took the napkin and dabbed her nose, blinking away the tears blurring her vision. "I'm sorry. This is none of your concern. If you…if you could take me to a phone, I'll call Harris and put an end to all this. You know what they say…try, try again another day."

"Try what?" Billy asked suspiciously.

A slow-motion tear rolled down her cheek. "What business is it of yours? Why should you care if there's a clock ticking in my life, if the sand is running out of the hourglass? The important thing is that I'm off your hands."

"There you go with the high drama thing again. What are you talking about? What hourglass?"

In a tiny voice, "Never mind."

"Look, Julie…I gave you a lift, no big deal. You're in a pickle tonight, and I don't think you're too familiar with pickles. Under the circumstances, I suppose I could give you a ride home."

"I may not know exactly where I am, but I know it's a good long way from my home in Palm Beach." She stopped sniffling long enough to stare at him suspiciously. "You haven't been completely thrilled with my company so far. Why would you want to go so far out of your way to take me home?"

Here Billy was on familiar ground. His former occupation had given him valuable experience in spur-of-the-moment fabrication. He leaned back in his seat, crossing his arms behind his neck. "Well, I didn't say the service would be completely free. I don't know if you're familiar with a cop's salary, but—"

"I understand." Julie looked at him, seeing something in his eyes she recognized only too well. Dollar signs. Finally, a situation she was adept at handling. "So I can have you for a price?"

Billy feigned shock. "I'm not that kind of man. You can hire my hired car for a price."

Julie tossed the hair away from her face, color flaming in her cheeks. She was magnificent, Billy thought wistfully, when she was truly offended. He experienced a surprising regret for what he knew he had to do.

"You know," she said tightly, "for a minute there I thought I was having a unique experience tonight. Silly me."

Billy lifted a brow innocently. "And you're not? Good heavens, woman, you learned to pump gas tonight. That could be a once-in-a-lifetime experience for a pampered princess like yourself."

"*That* was unusual," she replied cooly. "*You're* not, however. How much do vacationing policemen charge for putting on a Good Samaritan act? You don't come cheap, I imagine."

Billy was surprised at the conflicting emotions he felt. It appeared that at the advanced age of thirty-three, he was developing a late-blooming case of sensitivity. He didn't want her to think he was just another greedy opportunist, but the wide-eyed rich girl had to lose her fascination for the adventure she was having if he was ever to deliver her home. At that point, there would be no alternative but to leave Harris Roper's employment. The man was very clear about not wanting his little sister to know he was having her watched twenty-four hours a day. An unfamiliar face would have to be brought in if Harris wished to continue the invisible surveillance.

So, no matter how he looked at it, this was the beginning and the end of his contact with Julie Roper. The little word *end* had never pulled at him quite like this before.

"Just gas, princess," he said tonelessly, avoiding her wounded gaze. "And a little tip when I get you home wouldn't go unappreciated. Whatever you think I'm worth. Deal?''

"I hope you'll take a check," she bit out.

He forced himself to look at her, his smile stopping short of his eyes. "No problem. I think you're good for it. Dig out the map in the glove box and we'll find the quickest way to Palm Beach."

"Why bother? Drag it out and fatten your payoff." Her expression was uncovered briefly, showing the depth of her disillusionment. Quite softly she added, "You see, I do have an area of expertise. I'm very good at paying top dollar for what I want."

Billy closed his eyes briefly, fighting an urge to tell her how wrong she was. Of course, that would turn out to be a bad move as well, since he'd been on the Roper payroll long before he'd actually met Julie. Talk about a no-win situation.

He muttered a choice four-letter word beneath his breath and shoved the car into reverse, tires spitting gravel. His throat burned with the force of his frustration. Never in his life had he felt quite so helpless, and the feeling wasn't exactly warm and fuzzy. His jaw was clenched so tightly, his teeth ached.

"Whatever," he bit out. "Do up your seat belt. We're taking you back to Kansas, Dorothy."

Three

_____

He had a damn good excuse for getting lost.

That damn good excuse was sitting beside him, the breeze from the window scattering her spun-gold hair over the seat back. The air was redolent with her scent, a subtle combination of roses and baby lotion. Everything about her seemed magnified in the close confines of the car, the small sighs he heard now and again, her restless movements in the seat, even the faint shadows of weariness beneath her eyes. She had lost the urge to converse back at the gas station, keeping her thoughts and questions to herself. He couldn't blame her. He hadn't exactly treated her with kid gloves. Julie's face was turned away from him, her breathing slightly uneasy as if her silence was less than peaceful. He found himself stealing glances at her whenever he could, fascinated by this untried, defensive soul in his care. She seemed to be everything he was not: a delicate fantasy filled with curiosity, amazingly innocent and unguarded. Heaven knew there had been nothing like her in Oakland. Nothing like her in his entire life, actually. An hour into their drive, for reasons that evaded him, he'd turned the radio on softly, finding a melancholy blues station that seemed to fit his mood. And what a strange mood it was.

A pink chink in his scratched and dented armor? Maybe. Billy was, if nothing else, a realist, and knew it didn't matter at this point.

What did matter, he realized abruptly, was that he'd gotten them good and lost. Unless he'd been mistaken, the signpost he'd just seen half-buried in a cypress jungle read Gator Getaway, 5 Miles. Nothing at all about Palm Beach, no directions to freeways or interstates.

Damn. This was not going to reflect well on him.

"Did you see that?" Julie asked, breaking sixty minutes of brittle silence.

Billy feigned surprise. He was no different than any other man, and the words *I goofed* were not in his everyday vocabulary. "What? See what?"

"The sign we just passed. Gator Getaway…isn't that what it said?"

"Oh, *that* sign. I think it said, Gator, Get Away," some kind of a warning. I wouldn't worry about it." Then, hopefully, "Did you know you smelled like roses?"

"Don't try and change the subject." Julie grabbed the map and shoved it close to the dashboard lights. "What the…? Oh, it's upside down. Gator…Gator…There's nothing in the index called Gator Getaway. Are you sure you know where you're going?"

Cornered, Billy surrendered. "I am absolutely certain that I haven't a *clue* where we are, let alone where we're going. On the positive side, I know precisely where we've been. It's good to think positively, don't you think?"

"We're *lost,*" Julie said, with an equal mixture of alarm and satisfaction. "Ha! The boy wonder has gotten us lost. Lost, lost, *lost.* And now we're headed to some godforsaken place where alligators gather. What do you have to say about that?"

"Pick a four-letter word, any four-letter word. That's what I have to say about that." This city boy had no desire to visit a place where alligators congregated. If it weren't for the unrelenting darkness and swamp-like foliage, he might be able to get his bearings. This was not the way things were done in the concrete jungle. Roads *led* somewhere in California, and they weren't obscured by confusing walls of dripping, mossy vines. You might get stuck in a traffic jam, but you always knew *where* you were stuck, and you had colorful graffiti murals to enjoy while you waited. And if you happened to be an undercover cop, you could pull out the handy-dandy portable gumball machine, stick it on the roof of your car and zip down the emergency lane with cheerful impunity.

Not that a gumball machine would help him at this point. He had a sinking feeling he was already *in* the emergency lane.

"This is all your fault," he told Julie irritably.

Her jaw dropped. "What? What did you say?"

"You have no idea what you're putting me through tonight." He was not about to tell her how good she smelled or what incredible legs she had, although these things had certainly contributed to his mounting stress. "I'm coming unglued. I never got lost in California, never once. How do you people live in a wilderness like this? Where are all your stoplights? Where are your freeway entrances? I'd rather be dodging bullets in California than alligators in Florida, I'll tell you that. And that's if we're still in Florida. I have my doubts."

"Are you kidding? You don't know what state we're in?" Julie pressed her nose against the window, palms splayed over the glass. "I can't see anything," she whispered slowly. "No houses. No street lights, nothing. It's *never* dark in Palm Beach. Everything stays open all night. I'm really getting freaked out. Do something."

"What would you like me to do? Look, I'm only human. I can't read a map and keep us on the road at the same time. Florida is your state, I'm just a tourist. You're the one who is supposed to know your way around. You've lived here for…what? Twenty-five years?"

"Twenty-three years," she corrected stiffly. "Almost. And most of that time I was in England, anyway. Except for when I was in Italy. And the summers I usually spent in France or in the Hamptons, except when Harris insisted I go to finishing school in Switzerland, so—"

"How do you finish someone? I know how they do it in California, but how do they do it in Switzerland?"

"Well…you learn the social graces, and…never mind. Just trust me when I tell you my idea of finishing someone is probably quite different from your idea of finishing someone."

"I'll just bet it is. So you went to Switzerland to 'finish' yourself, but you don't know Florida any better than I do. This is just great. What the hell were you thinking tonight? The next time you decide to go for a joyride, hop on a bus and leave the driving to someone else."

Julie looked down her nose at him. "No wonder you were always getting shot. You have no manners whatsoever."

"Undercover cops are famous for that. They're so rude, people would rather shoot 'em than look at 'em."

"Well then, it's a shame you weren't a traffic cop. You'd probably be much nicer and you'd know something about reading a map and finding your way around. Your tip just went down, by the way.''

A moment of quiet passed before Billy trusted himself to speak. "Unfortunately for you, I was *not* a traffic cop. Now, since I've been known to have a temper and occasionally it gets the best of me, we'll just have a few minutes of silence.''

"We still don't—''

"Silence.''

Julie opened her mouth to retort, then looked sideways at his stark profile and thought better of it. There was something about the rigid set of his lips that suggested he had completely lost his sense of humor. As far as she could remember, she'd never witnessed a true testosterone temper tantrum. She had spent more time with Harris than any other man, and the closest he had ever come to losing his temper was loosening his tie. Strangely, some little devil within her *wanted* to see Billy lose his cool. She stared at him through a screen of lashes, inexplicably fascinated by the way his wild, wind-tossed hair moved over his hard brown cheekbones. There was a scar that cut diagonally through one dark eyebrow, perhaps a memento of yet another dangerous escapade. He was driving with hands at ten and two on the steering wheel, steely-blue eyes focused straight ahead and the speedometer glued to a steady forty-five m.p.h. Somehow she knew his emotions were barely in check. She was oddly intrigued by the notion of being the one to push him over the edge. She'd never wielded any sort of influence over men, particularly a man's man like Billy. He had a world of experience; she had none. And yet she had managed to get under his skin; she was at least savvy enough to know that. Was this, then, her first skirmish in the battle of the sexes? Had she won?

"Why are you doing that?" Billy asked suddenly, still staring straight ahead.

She looked away, squinting at the curtain of black nothing beyond the window. "Doing what?"

"Staring at me."

"How could you know if I was staring? You weren't even looking at me."

Quietly, "I knew. I know everything you do."

"Well…well…" Hells bells, this man had a way of overwhelming her. A few little words and her bravado evaporated beneath a nuclear flush. Had there been a referee in the back seat, round two would go to the hotshot from California.

"I don't want to talk anymore," she muttered.

"What do you know? Miracles *do* still happen."

Civilization was not far ahead. A sort of semi-civilization, at least. As far as Billy could see, they had landed themselves at some sort of amusement park/campground/motel combination. The flashing neon sign had every third letter burned out, but he was quite sure it read Gator Getaway. There were only two cars parked in the motel lot, one in front of the manager's office.

"Did you ever see *Psycho?*" Julie asked softly, brown eyes enormous. "This place is sort of scary."

"I worked undercover in California, remember? Nothing is more psycho than that. Besides, I can't drive any further tonight. I'm beat." Here again he was prevaricating. He could go without sleep for three days and never notice, but Harris Roper was a little more delicate. One way or another, Billy had to find enough privacy to call him. Not to mention the fact they were lost. It went deeply against his independent grain, but he had to ask someone where the hell they were and find out how to get where they were going. Billy shoved open his door and got out of the car, then, keeping in character, leaned down and lifted an eyebrow at Julie. "Unfortunately, I'm on a limited budget. You and your credit cards will have to check us in."

"Of course. I forgot for a minute you were the *employee*." Julie grabbed her purse and got out of the car, fighting an odd tightness in her throat. She followed Billy inside the motel lobby, sneakers stomping, then nearly ran back outside when she saw the clerk behind the desk.

There was no question about it. He bore a definite resemblance to Anthony Perkins, who played the knife-wielding motel owner in *Psycho*.

"We need a couple of rooms," Billy told him.

"Sorry," Anthony Perkins replied, stifling a yawn. "We're just about full up. We've got a single left, if that'll do ya."

Billy was half tempted to flip out his police badge, but since it was illegal, he liked to reserve that for emergencies. "As far as I could see, you have a dozen rooms and only one car parked in the lot. Did all those people come in one car?"

"Most everybody who visits us comes with a trailer and parks at the campground across the way. We only keep two rooms open during the off-season, and I just rented one of 'em an hour ago."

"Tomorrow won't do us any good," Julie told him, peering out from behind Billy's back. "We need it now. We'll pay double."

"You can pay double if you want, but my Margie only keeps two rooms clean in the slow season, and I ain't about to get her out of bed at three in the morning to make up another bed for the two of you. I got a single. You can have the single."

Julie was stupefied. In her somewhat limited experience, money had always insured cooperation. ''And if we pay you triple?'' she ventured.

The clerk blew out a frustrated breath and looked at Billy. ''Is she hard-of-hearing?''

''No,'' Billy sighed. ''She's rich, which is much worse. We'll take the single.''

Julie rounded on him. ''Hold on, buster. If you think for one minute—''

''I'll take the floor,'' he told her. ''Don't get your panty hose in a knot.''

''I'm not *wearing* panty hose,'' she threw back, her eyes flashing magnificently. ''And don't you dare be condescending to me.''

''Then you two aren't married,'' the motel clerk deduced, still looking at Billy. ''Congratulations, man. She's a stunner, but kind of uppity.''

''You don't know the half of it,'' Billy replied, grinning as he watched Julie's little hands clench into fists. ''All I did was try and help her when her car broke down, then first thing I knew I was saddled with a blond bombshell. And I mean *bombshell*.''

The clerk nodded somberly. ''Like in the war.''

''We'd like the room key,'' Julie snapped, slapping a credit card on the counter. ''And I would appreciate it if you would not talk about me as if I weren't here, thank you very much.''

The clerk shrugged and yawned again. ''Fine with me. I don't mind saying you're a little aggravating, lady. You folks will be in number three, just to your left as you walk out.''

''What did you say?'' Julie's chest was heaving beneath her designer gown. ''I am your *guest,* although you don't seem to comprehend that fact. For two cents I would contact my lawyer and—"

"Room three," Billy said, putting his hand over her mouth. "I've got it. Thank you. Sign the receipt, Julie. That's a good girl."

Julie signed, still making angry muffled noises beneath his hand.

"She's a regular firecracker, that girl of yours," the clerk commented. "I'll tell you what, she makes me appreciate my Margie even more. Here's your key, pal. You've got my sympathy, too."

Billy nodded, still grinning, still holding Julie's mouth firmly in check. He could feel her lips moving furiously against his palm, tickling his skin. "Thank you. Tonight I need all the sympathy I can get. Now I better get her out of here before she forgets her manners and bites me."

Julie's anger changed to numb disbelief the moment she walked into room number three. Although she was intimately familiar with four-star hotels, she had never visited a motel room before. The accommodations came as a shock. The room was small, smelled heavily of pine cleaner and had no furniture whatsoever beyond a bed, a small chest of drawers and a plastic lawn chair. No television, no wet bar, no chocolate truffle waiting for her on the pillow. There was, however, a grinning papier-mâché alligator nailed to the wall.

"This is so...*different*," she managed, unable to take her eyes off the alligator. "I've traveled all over the world, but I've never seen anything like this room before. Never."

Billy had been watching her closely, knowing this had to be a first for the pampered princess. Her soul-searing eyes were lavish with curiosity and apprehension, taking in everything all at once. Outwardly, Billy's manner was well-seasoned and somewhat amused; inwardly, his senses were prickling with sensual awareness. She was so damned beautiful, so endearing in her glittering dress and ridiculous high-topped sneakers. Her figure was petite and quite perfect, bright hair tumbled and rich against her porcelain-doll complexion. Every thought she had was reflected in her expression. She hadn't learned yet to hide it all, not like Billy had.

A first for him as well, he thought. After three or four hours she had him right where it hurt. No one had ever affected him with so little effort and so much force. With all his experience, he had no understanding of how this untried woman-child had managed it. His hooded gaze strayed to the single bed covered with a thin chenille spread. Mentally he slapped himself and looked at the broken curtain rod instead.

"I've been in worse," he commented.

She stared at him. "Good heavens. How much worse?"

"*Much* worse." He raked a hand through his hair, looking at the old-fashioned rotary telephone on the desk and wishing he could use it. It was time to face the music. His only chance of talking to Harris was the cell phone in his car. "Look, I'm going outside to lock the car up. I'll be right back."

"I'll go with you," she said immediately.

"I can make it on my own."

"I'm sure you can, but this is a strange place where they nail alligators to the wall. I don't like the idea of being alone in here."

"I thought you were high on adventures?" Billy retorted.

"I've had my quota for today," she replied. "Besides, I think you would be safe leaving the car unlocked." She bit her lip, the full impact of the recent emotional assaults catching up with her in one overwhelming wave of fatigue. "Don't you? We're not exactly in the South Bronx here."

It looked as if poor Harris would have to wait a little longer, Billy thought, looking at the shadows beneath her eyes. Given a choice between worrying about him or taking care of Julie, he knew Julie would always win. "All right. We'll catch some sleep. A few hours more won't matter at this point."

Julie's face clouded over. "What do you mean, a few hours more won't matter? Are you that anxious to get rid of me?"

Billy couldn't answer that one. For whatever reason, he didn't want to tell her yet another lie. The more time he spent with her, the less anxious he was to return her to the gilded cage. Not that it mattered. "Never mind. That wasn't what I meant. I do want to ask you something," he added, deliberately trying to distract her. "I don't mean to be nosy, but...do you always dress like that?"

"Dress like what?" Confused, she looked down at her dress. "What's wrong with it? It's Versace. You can never go wrong with Versace."

"I wasn't talking about the dress. What's with the sneakers? Are you trying to be a high-society trendsetter, or is it a grunge thing?"

Intrigued, she tilted her head to one side, her hair falling softly over her shoulder. "I changed from my heels before I left home. My feet were killing me. Tell me, what's a grunge thing?"

She was adorable. Billy stared long and hard, tiny smile lines etching his mouth and eyes. One moment she was a siren, albeit an innocent siren, the next she was a curious schoolgirl. She had a thriving interest in all things, a quality Billy found rare and irresistible. The thought came to him how very much he would like to be the one to answer her questions. *All* her questions.

"I really should go out to the car," he said suddenly, needing the cool air more than the privacy to call Harris.

"I told you, I'll go with—"

"Actually, I think I need a nice cold…uh, warm shower to help me relax before I hit the floor." He was fairly certain the bathroom was one place she wouldn't follow, and he needed time to remember who he was and what he'd been hired to do. He had the unsettling feeling that Julie needed someone to protect her from the man who was protecting her. "Do you need to—?"

"I'm fine," Julie said quickly. This sharing a room thing was more intimate than she'd realized, even when separate beds were involved. Bodily functions were not easy for a Palm Beach hermit heiress to discuss. "You just go right ahead. I'll…tend to things later."

Billy left her without another word, closing the bathroom door behind him with what seemed to be unnecessary force. Julie blinked the little room into focus, as if his absence put the strange spell she'd been under on Pause. She walked slowly around the room, picking up the Gideon Bible, reading a Gator Getaway postcard on the desk, bravely staring the wall alligator straight in the eyes. It certainly wasn't the Trump Tower. Odd, how it was growing on her.

She sat down on the bed, listening to the water running in the bathroom.

"Billy," she whispered, just to hear the sound of her voice saying his name.

She saw him in her mind's eye, his brown skin glistening with rivulets of water, his long dark hair swept back from his face, hard muscles beautifully defined with water, soap, light and shadow. Since her experience was very limited, her imagination was also, but she managed to do a fair bit of damage to her composure. She stirred fitfully on the bed, all too aware of the tension in her body. He was so far removed from the men she knew. There was an unmistakable sexiness to Billy, a raw masculinity mixed with a renegade boyish charm. His eyes were breathtaking when he smiled, the sunburst of tiny lines at the edges taking away ten years and a thick layer of cynicism. She closed her eyes and touched her lips, trying to relive the fleeting sensation of that accidental touch. It had given birth to an irresistible curiosity that grew with every minute she spent with him. She was feeling so much all at once, so many things awakening inside of her that were desperately needy and long-suppressed. And she knew somehow that it wasn't boredom, it wasn't simple restlessness taking her over. It was this man.

The shower was suddenly shut off. Julie scrambled back to reality, unlacing her sneakers, whipping off her dress, slipping beneath the sheets in her bra and panties. Billy came out of the bathroom with a towel slung low on his hips. His dark hair was wet and tangled over his forehead, a marked contrast to the silver-flecked brilliance of his eyes. He enveloped the room with the half-dangerous sensuality that had worried and pulled at her from the very beginning. For a moment she forgot the basics of breathing.

"You're all eyes, little girl," he said, attempting a light tone. "You look like poor Goldilocks in bed facing the bears. I hope I don't have to tell you—"

"You don't," Julie said quickly, pulling the covers up to her chin. "Of course you don't. I know I'm perfectly safe."

"Look, if I had something to sleep in—"

"Don't worry about it. I don't have anything on, and I'm just fine. I'm really—" a crack in her voice here "—comfortable. Well, I have *something* on. Don't misunderstand what I'm saying. I only took off my—"

"Let's not talk about what you've been taking off," Billy suggested tightly. He grabbed a blanket from the closet and shook it out on the floor. "Toss me the extra pillow, would you? Thanks. Now, let's get some shut-eye. Good night."

"Billy?"

He was already rolled up in the blanket like a cocoon, concentrating on not concentrating on Julie. "What?"

"Well…one of us has to turn off the light. If you'll close your eyes and promise not to peek, I'll—"

"You've got to be kidding me," Billy muttered, getting back on his feet with the blanket pulled around his shoulders. "We're not in sixth grade here. 'I promise not to peek' is not in my vocabulary." He padded over to the wall, putting his hand on the light switch.

Julie waited. Billy's hand remained on the switch, but the light stayed on. "What?" she said curiously.

Billy heaved a deep sigh and slowly turned his head, looking at her over his shoulder. His crystal-blue eyes were unblinking, his body still, a thoughtful furrow etched between his brows. He stared at her as if she were the most compelling and fascinating creature he had ever seen.

"I just wanted one more look at you," he said softly.

The room went dark. Julie heard him walk back towards her, then settle on the floor near the bed. Her breasts were heaving and her was skin prickling up and down her body, as if she was beginning to emerge from a chrysalis. No one had ever said anything like that to her before, completely without artifice or calculation. No words had ever had such a physical and emotional impact. She was caught; she felt as if she were lit from inside with something sparkling and fiery and sensual.

Sleep had never been so far away.

Four

In his past life, Billy Lucas had never had the time or the inclination to sleep late. Sleeping was boring…which was why he was so surprised when he opened his eyes to an obscenely bright and sunny room. He looked at his watch, blinking the digital reading into focus: 11:30 a.m.

Eleven-thirty?

The floor was harder than it had been when he had gone to sleep the night before. His back ached. His neck was stiff. He could feel tiny little groans from all four of his war wounds. He sat up slowly, knuckling his eyes. It never occurred to him that Julie might have awakened before he did, let alone that she might have showered and left the room without him knowing. No way. He had always slept lightly, like a cat. If anyone made a move, day or night, Billy would know it. That quality had served him well on many stakeouts.

Unfortunately, Julie's empty bed told him he had left

that quality behind in California, along with his career. The bathroom door was half-open, a wet towel lying on the floor. Billy felt sick, as if he had lost a dangerous suspect in his custody.

He scrambled to his feet and grabbed his jeans from the bathroom, hopping across the room first on one foot, then the other while he tugged them on. He was on his knees looking under the bed for his sneakers when Julie walked into the room. At least, he *thought* it was Julie.

She had the same eyes. Everything else was different.

She wore sandals, baggy khaki shorts and a cropped-off T-shirt that left her Florida-tanned midriff bare. A baseball cap was tugged low over her head, her hair swinging behind in a sassy ponytail. A brand new vinyl purse was slung over her shoulder. As far as Billy could see, every single thing she wore bore the less-than-famous logo of Gator Getaway.

"What are you doing down there?" she asked innocently. "Looking for me?"

"Very funny," he growled, getting to his feet. "I was looking for my shoes so I could start looking for you. You disappeared on me! I thought you were gone."

"I was—*duh.*" Brown eyes sparkling, she held up a clear plastic sack, stuffed with her sequined dress and sneakers. "This place is so *cute* in the daylight! It's like a really little Disneyland, only not so clean and with alligators instead of Mickey Mouse. Actually, they only have one ride, but they have a gift shop and they take American Express!"

"Don't you dare act like nothing is wrong!" Billy shook back his hair angrily, his expression fierce. Somewhere in the back of his mind, he knew he was overreacting, but he couldn't seem to put a lid on his temper. "While you were throwing your plastic around in mini-

Disneyland, did it occur to you that I might be wondering what the hell had happened to you?''

"Don't be silly. How could you be wondering anything while you were asleep?''

"Does it look like I'm asleep?'' Billy demanded. "Does it?''

"Not now,'' she said stiffly, losing her exuberant mood in a rapid free fall. "But twenty minutes ago when I checked on you, you were sawing logs like Rip Van Winkle. And twenty minutes before that, and twenty minutes before that. You sleep like the dead.''

"I am a policeman,'' Billy said, visibly offended. "I do *not* sleep heavily. None of us do. We are constantly alert!''

Julie dropped her plastic sack on the floor, crossing her arms over her chest. She didn't know quite what she had expected of him this morning, but it wasn't this. "That's ridiculous. Everyone needs to sleep, even policemen. I was beginning to wonder if you were in a coma.''

"Well, *if* I was sleeping heavily, it was because you completely wore me out last night.'' Billy played that back in his mind and winced. "I didn't mean that the way it—''

"Excuse me.'' Julie pushed her way past him, her lower lip slightly protruding. "I need to call Harris. I was waiting for you to wake up. No offense meant, Mr. Alert Policeman.''

"Harris?'' Immediately Billy switched channels. "Your brother? Wait. Not until I have a chance to…never mind. What are you going to tell him?''

Julie looked at him as if he had sprouted wings. "What is with you today? I'm going to tell him the truth, of course. I went for a drive, got lost, and ran out of gas. He'll send someone to pick me up. I've thought about it and I don't think I'll mention I spent the night with you. Harris might…have apoplexy or something. He's terribly sensitive where I'm concerned.''

Aren't we all? Billy thought. He was feeling incredibly guilty about taking the frosting off her cheerful mood, but she was the one who had disappeared on him. ''And when he asks where you are, you'll tell him…?''

''My brother's people are very efficient,'' she replied coolly. ''I guarantee they will be able to find me sooner or later. Now, if you'll excuse me for a moment…?''

''I have an idea,'' Billy said quickly, thinking hard and fast. ''Gator Getaway isn't exactly a tourist hotspot. If you wait for someone to find you, you could be here forever.''

''I know,'' she said, somewhat wistfully. Earlier this morning, she had fantasized about riding the rather rickety-looking Swamp Creature Carousel with Billy. What a shame it would be nothing more than a fantasy. ''That's okay. I can occupy myself.''

Billy felt yet another stab of guilt. ''Just tell your brother you're on your way home. We'll leave as soon as I shower. Then you'll be home twice as fast.''

She turned to face him, planting her hands on her hips. She forced herself to look only at his eyes, rather than at the fetching picture he made in the morning light. Bare-chested, hair tumbled from the pillow and blue eyes still lazy with sleep, Billy was a force of nature to be reckoned with. ''And of course you wouldn't have any ulterior motives, would you?''

''Hell and damnation.'' Billy threw his head back, staring at the ceiling for a good fifteen seconds. He hated this job more every minute. If he told Julie the truth, she would never forgive Harris. Or Billy, when it came down to it. *Oh, what a tangled web we weave…*

''We both know the deal,'' he said, mentally pulling

out his hair. "Gas and a tip. I've got a lot of time and trouble invested in you. Still, if you want to back out—"

"Fine. I just hope you can find your way to Palm Beach." Julie was close to tears, but she wasn't about to let Billy see. She turned back to the telephone, picked up the receiver and froze. The seconds ticked by. "This is rather unique. Is it an antique?"

"It's a rotary. And yes, it is sort of…antique."

Billy sighed heavily. He walked over to Julie, put his hands on her shoulders and gently moved her aside. "I'll dial. You talk. I have to earn my tip, after all."

Julie thought the call went well…at least, as well as it could have, considering Harris was unnaturally paranoid and hypersensitive. She told him she was just fine; he wanted to know if she'd been kidnaped. She told him she'd had car trouble; his voice went up a full octave, and he demanded to know if she'd been carjacked. Since his condition was worsening by the minute, Julie contented herself with telling him she was on her way home, safe and sound. She hung up before he could think of another dire predicament she might be in.

"Okay," she said, turning to Billy. "Everything's fine. He's reassured now. No problems at all."

"Oh, I'll just bet," Billy said dryly. "From what you've told me about your brother, I would imagine he's breaking out into a nasty rash about now. Will he have the FBI waiting for me when I bring you home?"

"I don't think so," she said doubtfully, chewing on her lip.

"What a wonderful morning." Sardonic humor glinted in Billy's eyes, and he looked Julie up and down, his gaze sticking like Velcro to her tanned, bare midriff. "You're quite the tourist today. Have you ever owned a plastic purse before? Or plastic shoes?"

"No." She looked down at her feet. "It's a first. I've had lots of firsts lately."

"Hey." Billy reached his hand out and tipped her chin up with a gentle finger. "The tip of your little nose is pink. Are you all right?"

"Of course I'm all right. Why wouldn't I be?" Now her eyes were swimming, darn it all, and she couldn't blink the tears away fast enough. "I mean, just because I can't find my way around Florida and can't put gas in my car and can't figure out how to use an antique rotary phone doesn't mean I'm some kind of an idiot. I'm just like everyone else in the world, right?"

Tenderness softened his expression. He shook his head and smiled faintly, allowing his finger to trace a soft line from her chin to the bottom of her quivering lip. "Julie, I can say this with complete and total honesty. You might be a little sheltered, but you are in no way, shape or form like anyone else in the world."

"Then you *do* think I'm some kind of an idiot."

"Shhh." He pressed his finger gently against her lips. "Do not babble while I'm talking. Let me finish. You are *not* some kind of idiot. You are unique. You are unpredictable. You are beautiful enough to break a man's heart at first sight. In short, little girl, you are some kind of amazing."

In a very small voice, "Oh."

"It's the truth," he said softly, relieved to be honest with her for once. He knew this was an opportune time to back off and head for another cold shower. At least, his head knew it. His body was telling him something else altogether. Without consciously making the decision, he allowed his finger to wander along the edge of her lower lip, fascinated by the full, satin-softness. He watched her gold-tipped lashes close and felt her softly exhaled breath against his fingertip. He knew he shouldn't be doing this. This was bad, very bad. He was getting paid to prevent everyone in the world from coming anywhere near Julie Roper. Obviously he wasn't doing a very good job of it. Someone should fire him. Immediately.

While his conscience squirmed, he continued to stare at her, head cocked to one side in a portrait of riveted curiosity. "Do you like that?"

"When you touch me?" Her beautiful pansy-brown eyes slowly opened wide, pupils dilated and free of any caution or fear. She didn't know enough to be afraid. "Yes. You're so gentle...it's almost like a kiss."

"My kisses," he said, fighting a tightness in his throat, "aren't always gentle."

"I wouldn't know." The words came out as a whisper. There was a sudden electrical charge in the space between their bodies, the air vibrating with the dangerous volatility of bottled nitroglycerin. Her eyes held his with unblinking intensity as she pressed her lips together, bravely pressing the lightest butterfly kiss on the tip of his finger. Just once, just once in her life she wanted to cross that damnable line of acceptable behavior. She had no idea what she was capable of feeling, but she knew Billy had all the answers to the questions she might have.

"Be good," Billy ordered, while at the same time his heavy-lidded, blue-glitter eyes drifted to her lips. "You know damn well you shouldn't..."

"I know. I shouldn't do this, shouldn't do that...." She stepped closer, her hips a whisper away from his. Her heart was pounding hard enough to jump out of her chest, but she managed something that she hoped was a smile. "I'm so tired of being told what to do. Didn't you ever want to do something just *because* you shouldn't? Because you were afraid this was your only chance, and you would regret it if you let the moment go?''

Billy closed his eyes tight. It didn't help; her image was burned on his retinas. ''No. Absolutely not.''

''You're lying.''

''You're playing with fire.''

''No, I'm not. I'm just...dancing around it a little.''

He sighed heavily, opening his eyes and drinking her in. A new, more intense flame flickered around his heart. She *was* beautiful enough to break a man's heart. And he was very afraid his was cracking around the edges. Gently, he said, ''Take off that damned hat.''

She did as she was told, her breath caught in her throat.

One side of Billy's mouth tipped up in a smile. ''Uh-oh. Suddenly you're doing as you're told. I should run for my life...but I won't.'' He dipped his head, rubbing the tip of his nose against hers. ''I can't.''

''Me, neither,'' Julie whispered inelegantly.

He buried his hands in her silky-cool curls, slanting his head sideways to catch her lips beneath his. It felt as though something had snapped in him, freeing the reckless, wild spirit he had been all his life. His mouth swooped over hers hungrily, abandoning gentleness in a desperate quest for some sort of physical satiation. She tasted like honey and roses and morning dew...and every other wonderful thing in life. He felt her gasp against his lips, then press her whole body against his with urgent wonder. Her hands were frantic, touching his shoulders and his chest and tangling in his hair, trying to find a way to hold him closer. His tongue lightly touched hers, and her body rippled with a hard shiver. Scary-shaky feelings quickly turned to scary-demanding feelings. Billy realized there *was* an experience in life he'd missed. He'd never kissed Julie Roper.

He lifted his head with a soft groan, resting his forehead against hers while he tried to get a grip on himself. His hands rested on either side of her face, his thumbs gently brushing the hot skin beneath her enormous brown eyes. A man could drown in those eyes, he thought. "I told you," he said, his voice thick and deep. "I'm not always gentle."

"I liked it." Julie hadn't the knack or desire for games. Besides, her heaving chest and trembling body gave her away. Once again she wrestled with that painful, persistent urging...*more.* "Did you...what was that like for you?"

"What was it like?" No one had ever asked him that before. Billy laughed softly, then tipped his head back on his neck and blew out a frustrated breath. "I can't...I felt...oh, hell. I'm not sure how to answer that without you slapping me."

"I wouldn't slap you," she told him with endearing earnestness. "You don't need to worry about that."

"Honey, if you knew what was good for you, you *would* slap me." Very deliberately he put both hands on her shoulders and pushed her a firm twelve inches away from him. "Get thee hence, Satan. This has got to stop." He started walking backward as he talked. "*That* was like going halfway to heaven, a place I never thought I'd visit. No, stay right there or I won't be responsible. *That* was like tasting ambrosia after starving for thirty-three years. *That* was a mistake, and I'm not sorry. Now I'm going to do the cold-water thing again. Excuse me."

The bathroom door slammed shut. Five seconds later it opened again. "Please don't go anywhere," Billy said. The expression on his face was a boyish, heart-lifting combination of tenderness, confusion and heat. "Just... stay there. I mean, here. Not here, in the bathroom, but here…close to where I am. I'm making a fool of myself, aren't I?''

Julie found herself a good solid wall for balance. It was all she could do to keep her knees from buckling. Her eyes were shining like dark stars, her lips still wet and slightly swollen from his kiss. She shook her head. ''No. You're just…babbling a little. Billy?''

''What?''

''I meant what I said. I liked it, too.''

So much was in his face: desire, longing, guilt, uncertainty. He stared at her without saying a word, stared at her until he was hot, bothered and hungry from head to toe. It was torture, he told himself, and he certainly deserved it. ''So…you'll be here?''

''I'm not going anywhere,'' Julie promised, hand over her heart. It was only after he'd shut the door that she smiled and said, ''Not on your sweet life.''

Gator Getaway looked much better in the daylight than it had in the dark. There were several campers parked behind the trees in the campground across the two-lane road. Beyond an incline behind the motel was a concrete pond ringed with black mud, a few straggly weeds and wire fences. The fences sported interesting hand-painted signs: Man-eaters! Critter Gumbo! Gatormania! Jumperoo Chicken Tossing!

''I wish I had a camera,'' Julie said in amazement, looking at the fat, mud-colored lumps in the pond that more than likely were alligators. ''Harris would never believe this. What do you think Jumperoo Chicken Tossing is?''

Billy looked sideways at her, grinning. ''More than likely chickens are involved in the tossing part and hungry gators do the jumperoo part. But that's just a guess.''

Julie shivered. "Are you serious? That's horrible. We can miss the chicken tossing, don't you think?"

"Absolutely. Someone has to stick up for the chickens."

They visited the booths and displays set up in three crooked rows, each and every one patterned with a swamp-creature motif. Julie had to investigate them all, fascinated by the variety of diversions. There was the Raccoon Break-a-Plate, Velcro Gator Wall, Snapping Turtle Ring Toss, Gator Spittoon Booth, Bungee Gator and Slingshot Frog Launch. It was like visiting a small county fair held deep in the bayou.

"I can't believe we're in Florida," Julie kept saying, sounding like wide-eyed Dorothy in The Land of Oz. "I didn't know places like this existed. Harris needs to see this. When I think of everything I've been missing stuck in stuffy old Palm Beach—"

"I doubt Harris would share your enthusiasm," Billy told her, visualizing Harris Roper's pristine white shirts and gleaming Italian shoes. It was the first time since kissing Julie he'd forced himself to think of the man and of the inevitable ending to this fairy tale. His smile lost some of its gloss. "From what you've told me about the man, he's too...tidy." He looked pointedly at the smear of mud on Julie's shirt, a proud memento of her attempt at crawfish roping. "Some people don't like to mix recreation with dirt. It ruins their fun."

"You know, I can't think of a time when I've seen Harris actually *having* fun. If he's not at work, he's worried about what might be going on at work. He even works on his laptop while being driven to the office. You'll meet him when we go back. I guarantee his ear will be stuck to a phone or his fingers glued to a keyboard."

Billy wasn't looking forward to "meeting" Harris. It would open up a whole new can of worms. Harris would be furious, Billy would be fired and Julie would be completely disillusioned and hurt when she realized how she had been deceived by both of them. Not a pretty picture, but Billy resolved to cross that shaky bridge when he came to it. In the little time he had left with Julie, he wanted to avoid thinking about the inevitable. *Just a few more minutes,* he told himself. *Then, I'll call Harris and put an end to…everything.*

Abruptly he said, "How do you feel about riding the Swamp Creature Carousel with a guy who has a weak stomach? Are you game?"

Julie laughed, looking at the slow-moving merry-go-round. "I was hoping you'd ask. Listen to how it creaks, like it's not going to make it around one more time. I'm game. I really don't think it moves fast enough to make anyone sick."

When the carousel halted to let two toddlers scurry off, Julie headed straight for a grinning alligator sporting a saddle. Billy followed slowly, eyeing the tiny plastic rowboat in front of the alligator and the pink baby hippo behind. He chose to retain some portion of his dignity and stand next to Julie, his chest brushing her shoulder, one hand on the white-painted pole that skewered her alligator through the middle.

"I'm scared," he explained.

"You're a chicken. You can't just stand here, you've got to *ride* something! What about the raccoon over there?"

"I'm allergic." He grinned as the ride started. "Too late now, anyway. It would be terribly dangerous if I let go of this pole."

"You big baby."

He jumped a little as the ride started. "I wasn't kidding when I told you I had a weak stomach. Going around in circles is not my favorite thing."

"I'll talk you through it," Julie soothed, her eyes sparkling up at him. "Just keep your mind on something else, Officer. Focus."

Focus, Billy thought. What an excellent idea, particularly when his subject was a very beautiful blonde, looking adorably sweet in her Gator Getaway outfit. Strands of sun-colored hair were dancing on her cheeks and shoulders with the curling breeze. Her smile was wide and completely unselfconscious, the smile of someone who was enjoying herself with complete abandon. Such a simple thing, a creaky little carousel. But to a privileged heiress from Palm Beach, it might have been a ride on the Concorde.

Julie had turned her attention to the only other passenger along for the ride, a towheaded little boy who was "driving" a miniature air boat. He was making noises as he drove, squeals, giggles and an occasional vrooooom.

"I love watching little children," she told Billy, raising her voice to be heard above the music-box tune the carousel played as it turned. "They're wonderful—not the least bit self-conscious. They let their imagination go wild, and they couldn't care less what anyone thinks of them." She looked up at him, her eyes dreamy and soft. "Wouldn't it be wonderful if we all followed our impulses without a second thought?"

"That depends," Billy said, "on whether you're a good guy or a bad guy."

She gave him a reproving look. "Stop being a policeman for five minutes. I'm talking about good guys, naturally. What if we were all like that little boy, enjoying every second and oblivious to the world and everyone in it? Don't you think that would be—'' she threw back her head and laughed as her ball cap went spinning off in the breeze ''—wonderful?''

''So you think we should all follow our impulses and not worry about how we might look?''

''Yes.'' She gave a dramatic sigh. ''In a perfect world, anyway.''

Billy's conscience started wriggling again. He knew what he was about to do, knew he shouldn't... and nothing was going to stop him.

''While we can,'' he said, ''let's pretend it's a perfect world.''

He leaned down, his lips catching Julie's soft mouth, parted with surprise. His kiss was fierce; like a condemned man eating his last meal. He tasted her with something akin to despair, dragging her with him into the erotic land far beyond her experience. He urged her lips to moist openness, feeling the unmistakable response that kicked his heartbeat into double time. Billy felt suddenly drunk, something that he *had* experienced before. He was also oddly afraid, something he had never experienced before. He was dizzy, he was angry at himself and he was hungry for more. The wanting never seemed to stop. He tried to imagine what it would be like when she was gone from his life. He couldn't, yet he knew it was coming. The surface of his skin felt as if he was standing too close to an open fire. Heads slanted, tongues danced, the world kept spinning and spinning....

When it was over, Julie could only gasp and stare at him, knowing for the first time in her life what it felt like to live her dreams. Billy was a man who had lost his innocence but not his charm. He knew all about the harsh realities of the world, yet somehow he had retained warmth and strength and gentle humor. Julie was being seduced by him inch by inch, she knew it as surely as she knew she was sitting on an alligator. He didn't seem to be doing it intentionally; he seemed to be doing it despite his better judgment. And he looked as surprised as she was.

"The ride's over," the teenage operator called. His freckled face was split in a jaw-cracking grin. "Has been for a while. Why don't you two get a room?"

The ride is over, Billy thought. *What a perceptive kid.*

"Oh, my sainted aunt." Face flaming, Julie scrambled off her scaly steed. "This must be one of the perils of giving in to impulses."

"One of them," Billy muttered. The other had something to do with snug-fitting jeans, but he wasn't about to go in *that* direction. They climbed off the carousel, Billy glaring at the smirking teenager as they walked through the gate. His mood was going downhill fast. "For two cents, I'd arrest you, kid."

Julie swallowed a nervous giggle and took his hand, pulling him along firmly beside her. "You can't arrest people for gawking. You're supposed to arrest the people being gawked *at.*"

"Then I would have to arrest myself," he replied, "and that would be really stupid. Where are we going, bossy woman?"

"To that picnic table under the tree." Julie took a deep breath, mustering her courage. "I have a proposition for you. It just came to me, like a vision."

"Oh, my sainted aunt," Billy parroted, not altogether in jest. Sweat broke out on his chest and between his shoulder blades. "Don't you dare. The way I'm feeling, I might just say yes."

"Not that kind of proposition. What kind of girl do you

think I am?'' She smiled over her shoulder, dragging him along with endearing awkwardness. ''I absolutely *adore* being able to say that. I've always wanted to.''

''Well, here's your answer. Soft. Rounded. Emotional. Beautiful. Wild at heart. Inexperienced but highly gifted. Gorgeous, silky lips—'' Belatedly Billy realized this was not a healthy topic of conversation between a bodyguard and his charge. ''Somebody hit me with a crowbar,'' he muttered. ''Can we just have a few minutes of quiet time? Just until I unscramble my abused brain?''

''You may,'' Julie said kindly, planting him on the wooden bench. ''I have something to say. There. Slide in, and I'll sit across from you. Don't look so terrified. This is a business proposition...more or less.''

Billy watched her with great suspicion. She was too animated, too bright-eyed and enthusiastic. He knew she had enjoyed the kiss as much as he had, but this went beyond a few mind-blowing minutes on a kiddie carousel. ''If your brother were here,'' he ventured warily, ''would he like this little proposition of yours?''

''If my brother were here,'' Julie pointed out reasonably, ''he would have hyperventilated and passed out cold when you kissed me. Hence, he wouldn't know anything about this little proposition. Stop worrying about my brother, Billy.''

''You don't understand. I can't stop worrying about your brother. Harris—''

''Harris,'' Julie interrupted, ''is not here and I am. Why are you so obsessed with him? He has nothing to do with anything.''

Except that he's footing the bill, Billy thought. *And I knew him long before I knew you.* ''You're wrong.''

"All right," Julie conceded, "that wasn't nice. Of course I'm concerned about Harris. That's why I'm going to call him immediately and tell him I'm not going home."

Five

Billy stared at her, his jaw slack. There were times, he thought, when he missed the comforting predictability of street punks. They'd been a piece of cake to anticipate compared to Julie Roper. "Would you run that by me again?"

Julie anchored herself with a sustaining breath, feeling as if she was standing very close to the edge of a precipice. The question of whether or not she could fly would never be answered until she stepped off the edge. "I realize this is an unexpected change of plans, but just listen. Since I'm temporarily cut loose anyway, there's no reason at all why I shouldn't give myself a few days of vacation. My birthday is coming up and…I find I need some time to reflect…there are some decisions I've been putting off, and…well, you're not interested in that. The long and the short of it is that I'm not quite ready to go home yet."

"Why? You know damn well you have to go home.

Home is where you belong.'' Then, in a completely different tone, ''What decisions?''

''It's sort of private,'' Julie evaded, looking sideways and twirling a tendril of hair around her finger. ''At least…now is not the most opportune time to tell you the specifics. You'll have to trust me on this. Your mood has suddenly turned sour.''

''What has *my* mood got to do with anything? You're the one with the sudden urge to take a vacation. And you're the one with the super-sensitive workaholic brother pulling out his hair at home. Do you want to put the poor little guy in an early grave?''

''How did you know he was little?'' Julie said, temporarily distracted.

Billy winced, painfully aware he'd blown his cover like a fresh-faced rookie. He could hardly tell her he'd met Harris for the first time nearly a month earlier, all five foot eight inches of him. He remembered thinking a strong breeze could do a lot of damage to the fellow. ''He sounds little,'' he said stupidly. ''You're always talking about poor Harris like he's fragile.''

Julie was too preoccupied with her ''proposition'' to notice Billy's barely disguised discomfort. ''Oh. Well, he *is* kind of thin, but that's because he has so much nervous energy. I love my brother, and I know only too well how much he worries about me. Which is why—'' another deep breath here ''—I would like to offer you a job as my bodyguard. No, no…just listen for a minute. I'm being very honest with you when I say I've never enjoyed myself so much in my entire life, even when we fight. In my circles, not a single soul openly argues with anyone else. If a disagreement pops up, if someone becomes irritated with someone else, they call their lawyers and sue each other. It's all very civilized.''

"Oh, that's *just* what I want to talk about this morning," Billy muttered. "Lawsuits. I suppose your brother has more than his share of attorneys on the payroll?"

"Scads of them. What does that have to do with anything? Pay attention. When I ran away last night, I was really confused about…all kinds of things. But today… everything is much clearer. I've realized there are a few things I need to do before I go home. I have a wish list. Not a real list on paper, because if Harris happened to see it he would hyperventilate—"

"And pass out cold. I know. Go on."

Julie looked furtively to the right and left, as if to reassure herself Harris wasn't standing behind the nearby tree. "Everyone I know treats me like spun glass. I don't know if they're more worried about me or about poor paranoid Harris. But you…Billy, when I'm with you, I'm just an ordinary woman, no different than any other woman."

You couldn't be more wrong, Billy thought. "This suspense is killing me," he said quite truthfully. "Cut to the chase. What's your proposition?"

"Before I go home I'd like to do a few things I've never done before and always wanted to do. I'd given up hope that this would ever happen, but you've changed that. You obviously don't try to impress me just because I have a rather obscene amount of money. You have no idea how refreshing that is. I don't have to watch everything I say and do. And you're experienced with… criminal types and whatnot, so you'd be an ideal choice for my vacation bodyguard. I could completely relax and concentrate on making the most of the time I have left."

"The time you have *left?*" Billy sat up very straight, his eyes boring into her. "What the hell does that mean? Are you sick or something?"

"Oh, no. Not exactly. I'm just…facing a sort of deadline."

Billy had long ago perfected the art of spotting true guilt, regardless of how well it was disguised. She was drenched in it. Very softly, he asked, "What deadline, kiddo?"

"My birthday," she said, chewing on her lip.

"You're not old enough to dread birthdays. Why don't you save me a lot of trouble and just spill the whole thing? I'll get it out of you one way or another. You'll just have to trust me on this."

"Mmmm." Julie twisted uncomfortably on the wooden bench, wincing as a sliver rose up to greet her. "Why couldn't you have been a travel agent or something instead of a cop?"

"Spill it."

"Okay, okay. I'll be twenty-three a week from Friday. I have this friend who thinks that would be a perfect day to…to…formalize things. Or at least become engaged to eventually formalize things."

Billy focused on one word of her rambling explanation. "Engaged? As in *engaged?* To be married?"

"He asked for my ring size. I knew it was coming, but…you know, he's really very sweet. His name is Beauregard James Farquhar III. Our families have known each other forever. Harris likes him very much." Julie realized there was a terrible breach of etiquette in the timing of her confession. She had enthusiastically kissed Billy not five minutes earlier. She had enthusiastically kissed him two hours before that. Now she was telling him about Beau and her birthday and the complications waiting for her at home. If there was a proper way to do this thing, they hadn't explained it at finishing school. "Harris likes him very much," she repeated lamely.

Apparently the marine sergeant look-alike Billy had seen her with was more than a friend. His mood free fell from sour to slightly homicidal. He stared at her for what seemed to be an eternity. "And what about Julie? Does *she* like Bo-Bo-the-Third?"

"His name is Beau, and of course I like him. He's like…he's like white bread, there's nothing *not* to like. He's very careful about that. Look, I know this seems really strange to be telling you this, especially after…"

A little muscle was working hard and fast in Billy's jaw. "After what? Sharing a couple of kisses? Honey, kisses aren't contracts. They're not even contracts to be engaged to eventually formalize a contract."

"There's no need to be sarcastic." Billy's unrelenting, hard-eyed scrutiny had taken her to a new level of embarrassment and confusion. "I know the situation is a little complicated, but I'll work it out. I've known Beau since my diaper days. My parents knew his, his grandparents knew mine. Everyone has always assumed we would get married. Harris looks at it like the end of his parenting sentence. He trusts Beau and knows he would never hurt me. He might even get himself a life of his own once he isn't preoccupied with mine."

Billy's gaze was as clear and chilling as a winter sky. "So go the hell home and marry Bo-Bo. Problem solved, everyone lives happily ever after." Almost everyone.

"Will you stop calling him that? I don't know if I want to marry anyone. The only thing I do know is that I'm not ready to go back to my life. I have no idea who this girl is wearing these silly clothes and having all these adventures, but I'd like to find out." She gazed at him earnestly, willing him to understand. "I *have* to find out, don't you see? I'll do this one way or another, with you or without you."

"Sit right there, please," Billy said with deceptive calm. He got up from the table and slowly paced a wide circle around it. Julie's head twisted on her neck like a wary owl's as she watched him. Once, twice…three times around, and he still couldn't put a name to the crazy uproar in his mind.

The existence of Bo-Bo-the-Third had taken him completely by surprise. Harris had never mentioned the man. Billy had assumed Julie was unattached. And why?

Probably because he wanted it that way. And when it came to the fairer sex, Billy Lucas usually found it rather easy to get what he wanted.

He tried to revert to a policeman's cold calculation. One, he was hired to protect her, not fall for her. Two, she was engaged to be engaged. Three, he knew her well enough to realize she was quite serious about not going home right away. He could either let her go it alone or tag along and try to keep her out of trouble. Either way, Harris wasn't going to like it.

And either way, Billy lost. He'd bungled the bodyguard job big-time when he'd let himself get emotionally involved. He wasn't about to look too closely at his feelings, not when he knew he stood on such shaky ground. East was east and west was west, and Palm Beach was on a different planet than both. A former cop with a missing reprobate for a father was no match for Bo-Bo-the-Third, who no doubt sported a pedigree like a champion Maltese dog.

When he finally stopped pacing and looked at Julie, his expression was deliberately obscure. His cop face. "I'm expensive," he said.

Julie blinked, taken aback by his coldly detached manner. Whatever she had expected of him, it wasn't this.

"All right. Since I'm probably ruining your vacation, I want to make it worth your while." She waited, wanting him to tell her she was wrong, that he enjoyed being with her. He didn't.

"Just so you're warned. On the plus side, I'm good at what I do, so you'll get your money's worth, and Harris will get you back safe and sound." He sat down again, smiling at her across the table. "And just to set the record straight…I hope the fact I kissed you a couple of times isn't the reason you're putting off going home. Because that's all it was, kiddo—just a couple of kisses. You and Bo-Bo sound like you're meant for each other. I'm not even in the equation, beyond being the hired help."

"Of course." Julie stared down at her tightly folded hands, wanting desperately to hide the unexpected hurt his words inflicted. It took her a moment to control and relax the burning muscles in her throat. "I'm not a child, Billy. I told you in the beginning, this is a business proposition."

"And you'll let your brother in on all this, right?"

"Of course." A pause. "Most of it. If I tell him exactly where I'm going, he'll show up and smother me to death. I'll just reassure him that I'm fine, I've hired someone for security and I'll be back in a week. He'll be okay with that."

"I don't think so," Billy told her flatly. "I don't think he'll understand at all. *I* don't understand. What are you looking for, Julie? What could you possibly need that you don't already have?"

Softly, "This isn't about what I need. It's about what I want. There's a big difference."

Billy shrugged, hating the wounded expression on her face and hating himself for putting it there. For some odd reason he remembered something his mother used to say to him when he needed to be punished: This is going to hurt me more than it will hurt you. "Whatever. Where are we going on this little excursion of yours?"

"I'll let you know," she said. She looked up at him, taking an iron hand to her emotions. "You're being paid. That should be the only thing that really concerns you, right? The money?"

He forced himself to smile. "Bottom line every time. That's what happens when you're not born into the privileged class."

"Whatever," she said, imitating his careless indifference. She got up from the table, shoving her hands into the pockets of her shorts and looking at him with thorny dignity. "You'd think I'd be used to it by now, wouldn't you?"

"Used to what?" Billy asked.

"Being different. Every now and then I make the mistake of feeling like an ordinary person, no one special. Then reality hits, and I realize just how valuable I am. I'm going to call Harris, then the airline to make some reservations. In the meantime, you go to the office and check us out."

The last sentence was obviously an order from employer to employee. Billy gave her the small victory. The starry-eyed woman-child was hurting, though she was trying valiantly to disguise it. Comforting her was out of the question. Explaining anything to her was out of the question. Harris was her only family, and Billy didn't want to harm their relationship in any way. If they could somehow muddle through this fiasco without Julie knowing who had actually hired Billy in the first place, it would be for the best.

At the moment, checking out of the motel was the only option Billy had.

"Yes sir, ma'am," he said, sketching her a little salute. "Anything else?"

She raised one eyebrow. "Are you going to have an attitude now?"

"No sir, ma'am."

"That's good. Oh, and ask the motel clerk for the number of the local police so we can report the Porsche as stolen." Abruptly she turned on her heel and strode towards the motel without another word.

Billy understood better than she what was happening between them. He couldn't afford to indulge her romantic fantasy, regardless of how appealing it was. He didn't much care what happened to him, but he did care what happened to Julie. It had nothing to do with money or his professional responsibility, not any longer.

It was personal now.

Julie booked them on the airline ticket as Billy and Julie Roper. She had completely forgotten she still didn't know his last name. Odd...it had simply never occurred to her to ask. He was Billy and she was Julie, no surnames, no biography, no past or future. The present had been all that mattered. And now that the adventure had taken a less romantic turn, it was probably best left that way. They turned in the Rent-a-Wreck at the airport, boarding the plane with only five minutes to spare. Julie carried no personal items other than her vinyl purse and the Versace gown stuffed in a plastic sack.

Her mood was fluctuating between anxiousness, apprehension and excited curiosity. She was also experiencing an overwhelming surprise with herself that doubled and redoubled itself every minute. She had actually carried out her plan, embarking on an adventure willy-nilly, with no second-guessing. She had no idea whatsoever what Billy might be feeling, as he was uncharacteristically withdrawn. She watched him sitting beside her when he wasn't looking, wondering what he was thinking and not willing to break the standoff and ask.

For his part, Billy was so frustrated he wouldn't have been surprised if steam was coming out of his ears. He'd managed to sneak away from Julie at the airport, calling Harris from a stall in the men's room. With a wary eye on the Low-battery light on the cell phone, he talked rapidly, touching on the highlights of Julie's nocturnal flight. He promised Harris he would bring her home safe and sound…and the battery went dead. Harris hadn't had a chance to say more than two words. One was "damnation," the other was "immediately." Harris was not a happy camper.

"Why aren't you talking?" Julie asked at thirty thousand feet.

"I didn't plan on going home to California for another two weeks. Why Los Angeles?"

"We have a place in San Clemente," Julie replied, relieved to put an end to the thick silence. "I decided it would be a good home base."

"Home base?"

"A starting point," Julie told him, hesitant animation lighting her eyes. "A place to stay during our escapade. I've only been there a couple of times myself, but it's really comfortable, and located very strategically. They say that everything you want in the world you can find in California."

"What about Harris? We both know he'll come looking for you. Don't you think he'll check your home in San Clemente sooner or later?"

Julie considered this, frowning. "Well…I hadn't thought of that. I suppose if he does, he does. Still, my mind is made up. With or without Harris looming over me, I'm going through with this. For seven days I'm a free woman, come hell or high water."

"So what did he say when you called him?" Billy had wanted to ask her long before now, wondering if he was on the FBI's Most Wanted list. Given Harris's penchant for overreacting, he figured it was only a matter of time. "Did you tell him about me?"

"Of course. He was a little…unsettled when I told him about my vacation, so I tried to put his mind at ease. I told him I'd hired a bodyguard. I said he would be with me night and day."

Billy winced. "And what did he say to that?"

"I don't know," Julie said quite honestly. "I told him we had a bad phone connection and I hung up. I'll call him again in a couple of days."

Billy sighed and leaned his head against the seat back. He read the little sign overhead: In case of emergency, the oxygen mask will automatically drop down. He felt like he could use a little oxygen right now. At some point in the past couple of days, he had lost control of his life. Now he was riding in Julie's tumultuous wake, trying desperately to stay afloat.

"I'm your bodyguard," he said, still staring at the oxygen-mask sign. "So I figure it's my job to make sure you get your space. If your brother is as protective as you claim, he'll probably have someone check the place in San Clemente. I have a better idea." He turned his head towards her, meeting her eyes fully for the first time since boarding the plane. "I have a buddy who owns a weekend place in Laguna Beach. I have a key and an open invitation. I use it whenever I want a freebie vacation. Would that suit your mysterious plans, whatever they may be?''

"Laguna Beach? I've never been there. What's it like?''

He smiled faintly. ''I doubt the house is as extravagant as your home in San Clemente. It's just a little cottage dug into a hill above the beach. You'd like the village, though. It's an artists' colony, kind of like an upscale, year-round outdoor fair.''

"A fair?'' Julie's face lit up. Like Billy, she leaned back in her seat, giving him a dazzling smile that pulverized his heart. ''Really? I've never been to a fair. That sounds wonderful. Would your friend mind? What if he's using it?''

"Colin is a cop and knee-deep in a murder trial for the indefinite future. I can pretty much guarantee he won't be using it. At any rate, I'd rather he show up than Harris. Colin is a great addition to any party. As a matter of fact, Colin kind of *is* a party. I'll introduce you someday—'' He stopped, catching himself. ''Or not. I keep forgetting my place, don't I?''

"That's ridiculous.'' Julie touched his arm, wanting nothing more than to erase the cold front that had moved in between them. ''Look, I know I might have come across as being a little stuck-up earlier. I'm very sorry. You just have a way of bringing out the worst in me.''

"I try,'' he replied, one side of his mouth tipping up in a smile.

"We're going to be spending a lot of time together, so I promise to be on my best behavior. We'll pretend we just met, and I'll act exactly like they taught me in finishing school. Rule number one—when meeting new people, do not talk about yourself. Instead, ask about their background and interests. Where are your people from?''

Billy's smile dropped like a rock. "My people? There you go, sounding stuck-up again. Did they teach you in finishing school that some people might not enjoy talking about themselves?"

Julie shrugged helplessly, having no idea what she'd done to suddenly turn him into the growling, undercover cop again. "And there *you* go again, being rude. I'm doing my best to—"

"Julie Roper?" This was a new voice, a female voice dripping with an affected drawl. Both Julie and Billy's heads swiveled simultaneously, eyes locking on the woman who stood in the aisle next to their seats.

"I don't believe my eyes," Julie said, in the same tone she would have used had she spotted a mouse running about the plane. "Marie Claire. What a terrible—uh, a what a terrific surprise. Fancy running into you way up here in the sky."

Billy gave Marie Claire a single, sweeping look, identifying and tagging the fortyish redhead immediately. Species: rich, nosy and affected socialite. Icky, very icky.

"Darling girl," Marie Claire gushed, bending down to give the air next to Julie's face a kiss. "Precious, *adorable* girl, whatever are you doing in business class? I stuck my head around the corner, and there you were. 'Why, that's Julie Roper,' I said to myself. I just had to come and say hello. If I'd known you were on the plane, I would have insisted you sit with us in first class. Unless you're with someone already…?" She looked pointedly at Billy. "A new friend?"

"How are you, Marie Claire?" Julie replied, trying to gloss over the question. "Is Louis with you?"

"Darling, no." Marie Claire placed her hand over her heart as if preparing to recite the Pledge of Allegiance. "Feel for me. I'm trapped up front with Danielle Devereaux, can you imagine? I swear to you, she never stops talking. She's arranged a show for her latest pet artist at Galleo's in Los Angeles, and we're flying out for the opening. You must come." Then, without missing a beat, she turned her scarlet-rimmed smile on Billy. "And any guest you'd like to bring, naturally. I hope I didn't interrupt. And you would be…?"

I would be sick to my stomach, Billy thought, revolted by the woman's affectations. He was also revolted by her hat, which loomed over them like a pink flamingo with wings outstretched. It was enormous, heavy-laden with what appeared to be perfectly trimmed pink bonsai trees. The sheer weight of a hat like that could cause spinal injuries.

"My name is Billy," he said. When she waited for him to continue, he stared at her blankly. "What? Do I have something in my teeth?"

"Heavens. Of course not." She tittered, looking back at Julie. "Isn't he interesting? Have you known each other long?"

"Just since the plane took off," Julie said, painfully aware of the sharp gaze Billy turned in her direction. "I'm traveling alone."

"Well, of course you are," Marie Claire said, patently relieved. "I don't know what I was thinking. Beau is such a darling, and the two of you are priceless together. Will he be joining you?"

"No."

"Harris, then?"

"No. I'm just going to do a bit of shopping, then fly home first thing tomorrow. You know what that's like when you have a man tagging along. Such a bore. It's been lovely seeing you, though. Give my love to Danielle."

"Of course. And we'll see you on the sixteenth. Your birthday party sounds absolutely marvelous. Of course, Harris never does things halfway, does he? I'll call you when I get back home, darling. We'll try out that new bistro on Lighthouse Point." She leaned forward, lowering her voice confidentially. "Darling, I have to compliment you. Your clothes…so outrageously original. Flirty and fun, and so amusing! New designer?"

Julie looked down at her Gator Getaway crop top, biting down on a smile. "Yes, but I'm keeping him to myself. It's so hard to find anything unique."

"I don't blame you," Marie Claire said. "Guard your secret, darling. If the word got out there was a hot new talent, simply everyone would be wearing his clothes. Where's the fun in that? Bye-bye, then! Safe trip home."

The woman and her hat went back to first class from whence they had come, bonsai trees bobbing. "Talk about bad luck," Julie told Billy, striving for a light tone. "Of all the planes in the world, we had to pick the one Marie Claire was on."

"But it must have been *agonizing* for you," Billy said, imitating Marie Claire's over-emotional delivery. "The first time you travel business class, and someone has to see you. Not only that, but you're seated next to a man who simply isn't up to snuff or you would have introduced us."

"How was I supposed to do that? I don't even know your last name."

"*What*-ever. Would you like me to move to another seat, *darling?*"

"This is not my fault. If I'd told her we were traveling together, she would have grilled you like a salmon. Marie Claire has to know everything about everyone. I was trying to spare you, not to mention get rid of her as quickly as possible.''

"And I'm sure it had nothing to do with Bo-Bo, right?''

Julie shrugged helplessly. ''She happens to be Bo-Bo's...Beau's aunt. I just thought it would be easier to keep things as simple as possible, for you and for Beau.''

"Protect little Bo-Bo if you like,'' Billy said in a silky, dangerous voice. ''But don't you dare put me in the same category. I'm nothing like the people in your world.''

"I know,'' Julie whispered. ''That's why I'm here, Billy.''

He was sensitive to the shaky wave of emotion in her voice. Marie Claire, Bo-Bo and the rest of the world went on spinning, while Billy stepped off the ride and fell into her eyes. It was incredible; the overwhelming longing that came so quickly. Nothing had ever felt more real than the primeval magic she stirred in him. It didn't seem to matter if he was angry or frustrated or confused—the need remained with him like the haunting underscore of a sweet, sad song.

"Lucas,'' he said softly.

Her dark gaze drifted over his mouth. ''What?''

"My last name...it's Lucas.'' He studied her with somber intensity, his senses flooded with her ethereal, spring-like scent. He experienced an inkling of how murderously difficult the next few days would be. He sympathized deeply with himself. ''And unless you want to be embarrassed in front of all these business-class people, you'd better get that look out of your eyes.''

Six

It was long past sunset when they landed. The stress of the past two days was telling on Julie; the faint pallor of her skin evidence of a soul-deep weariness. She walked in whatever direction Billy pointed her, giving a soft sigh of relief when they were ensconced in yet another rental car.

"I wish it wasn't dark," she sighed, stifling a yawn with a ladylike pat of her hand. "I wanted to see everything. Usually when I'm in California, I see only the inside of a limo and the back of the driver's head. And Rodeo Drive in L.A. I know that area pretty well."

"She shops on Rodeo Drive," Billy muttered. "I shop at All-a-Dollar. Talk about being in over my head."

Either she didn't hear him, or she chose to ignore him. "I need to buy some clothes first thing tomorrow. And makeup. And I should buy a camera. I want to take pictures of absolutely everything."

"A little scrapbook for Harris," Billy replied, thinking it would be very good evidence for the man to submit at the trial when he sued Billy. "How nice."

"Speaking of clothes…" Julie turned a puzzled gaze on him "…where are yours? You didn't check any luggage at the airport."

That's because everything is back at your house in Florida, Julie. "I can wear Colin's stuff while I'm here. That way we didn't have to go back to Miami for my bags."

She was too tired to ask where in Miami, what the hotel would think when he didn't return, etc., etc. Billy was grateful for this. The happy lack of conscience he had enjoyed as an undercover cop was getting harder and harder to tap into. Every lie he told, he realized, he would have to take responsibility for sooner or later. He awaited that day with the same anticipation he would have shown for a root canal.

"Okay," she said vaguely. "This friend of yours, Colin. Do you two work together?"

"Used to," Billy replied, happy to divert her attention to something harmless. "Unfortunately, he got demoted to a humble patrolman a couple of months ago. Colin has a temper, and it got the best of him during a drug raid. So now he's back in blue, with a nifty new crew cut." Billy grinned, remembering the shouting match in the captain's office when Colin had been ordered to lose his prized ponytail. "He looks like a poster boy for the marines now. It's killing him."

"Are the two of you close?"

"Like brothers. We're both rebellious nonconformists, so we bonded from the beginning. We've always said we would have been very successful criminals had we not chosen to work for Truth, Justice and the American Way.''

Julie feigned shock. ''There's *two* of you?''

He smiled, watching her eyelids grow heavy. ''Scary, isn't it?''

Julie tried to stay awake—it seemed she was doing a lot of sleeping in cars the past couple of days—but long flights had always given her jet lag, and jet lag usually translated into a prompt semi-coma. The last thing she remembered was the soft sound of Billy's fingers thrumming on the steering wheel, jamming with Springsteen. ''Badlands.'' What an appropriate song for her nonconformist…rebel…

''You're so…I love the way you…'' she yawned, head drooping against the seat.

''Oh, no, you don't.'' Billy nudged her with his elbow. ''What? If you were going to say something nice to me, wake up. Julie? I'm so what?''

Julie's dream-hazed mind somehow translated the elbow prodding her side to a massage at the Golden Door Spa. ''Let's do a seaweed wrap, Aristotle,'' she said quite clearly. ''And I'd adore some peach juice.''

''Seaweed, schmeeweed,'' Billy muttered. ''And who the hell is Aristotle?''

''We're here, Sleeping Beauty. Wake up.''

Once, twice…Julie's lashes fluttered open on the third try. Through the windshield, she saw a garage door. Nothing else, just a garage door. ''Where's the rest of the house?'' she mumbled.

''On the next floor.'' He grinned as she sat up, rubbing the small of her back. ''You have a big old wrinkle in your face.''

"And I have a big old kink in my back. Why are we sitting here with the car idling?"

"We're waiting," Billy explained, unable to take his eyes off her. Her hair was glowing white-gold around her face, a little angel halo that was at odds with her slightly disgruntled expression.

"What are we waiting for?" she asked.

He disciplined a smile. "For the door to open."

"Well, it's not opening. The electronic beam must be…" Her voice trailed off as she exchanged a look with Billy. "There is no electronic beam, is there?"

"No, ma'am. We're slumming it. It's manually operated."

When Billy moved to open the door, she told him to stay put. She climbed out of the car, lifting the heavy aluminum door as if she had been doing it all her life. Illuminated in the headlights like a stand-up comic, she whirled towards Billy and clapped enthusiastically for herself. "It was easier to deal with than the rotary phone," she called out. "I have great potential for becoming an ordinary woman."

"Not a chance, lady," Billy whispered, unable to take his eyes off her. Her magnificent eyes were flashing with renewed energy and her lavish smile was enough to break a former undercover cop's heart. His little adventuress had come to sunny California with nothing beyond a Gator Getaway toothbrush and the clothes on her back. She didn't seem too worried about the fact, either. His eyes lingered on the soft fullness of her breasts beneath the thin T-shirt she wore, then drifted lower to her bare midriff. The car continued to idle. And idle.

The adventuress planted her hands on her hips. "What?"

Billy spared a moment's gratitude for the shadowed

interior of the car. An instant sunburn heated his face as he drove carefully into the garage. He gave himself a second to cool down, lowering his window and directing Julie to a light switch near the back door.

"I know," she grinned over her shoulder, still plucky and positive despite the long day. "It's not motion sensitive, right?"

Billy walked ahead of her into the house, turning the lights on one by one. The floor above the garage was small but cozy: a kitchen, living room and dining room all rolled into one. Thankfully, it looked as though Colin had hired someone to clean after his last visit. A trace of pine cleaner still hung in the air, along with the stronger lemon scent of room freshener. The plush carpet was vacuumed free of footprints, the pillows on the sofa plumped and neatly arranged and a variety of magazines fanned out on the coffee table. Definitely not Colin's work, Billy thought. When in residence, Colin decorated with beer cans, pizza boxes and newspapers.

Beyond the spotless glass sliding doors was a small redwood deck overlooking the ocean. Julie could make out a hammock on the deck, along with several hanging flower baskets. Beyond, the ocean gleamed with a strange, shimmering tinfoil color.

"It's overcast tonight," Billy said, watching her as she stood motionless in front of the glass. "You won't be able to see much until morning. I suppose we could walk down to the beach if you'd like…?"

Julie shrugged, still smiling at him. "In the morning. I forgot you were driving while I was sleeping. Where do we…where do you sleep? And where do I sleep?"

Smiling at her careful little question, Billy led her to the top floor where the master bedroom and bath was located. The room was decorated in crisp tones of beige, white and black, again offering a balcony beyond the sliding glass doors. The bath was enormous, a walk-up Jacuzzi in the corner beneath a huge, stained-glass skylight. It was also the only bedroom.

"Just one bedroom," Julie murmured. Her thoughts couldn't have been plainer if they'd been written on her forehead with black permanent marker.

"The sofa downstairs," Billy told her gently, "pulls out into a bed. There's also a guest bath downstairs, so you'll have complete privacy. Did you really think this was going to be a problem?"

"I wouldn't be here if I did." It was the strangest thing, but Julie felt as if she had known him forever. They connected on a level she had never experienced before, no matter how unusual their circumstances. Although she couldn't explain it even to herself, she felt as if she could see into his heart. He had proven himself to be a gentleman, far more so than many of the "gentlemen" Harris had introduced her to. Those poor, self-absorbed fellows grew prematurely old worrying about money, and they couldn't seem to distinguish between valuables and valuable. Never had their inner resources been truly tested, and heaven help them if they had. In choosing the profession he did, Billy no doubt had faced the ugliest side of life. If he had been emotionally deadened by those experiences, she had yet to see evidence of it. For all his posturing about money and his lack thereof, she couldn't help noticing a softness to his hard-edged persona. Oh, he was male through and through, but his beautiful blue eyes were still amazingly gentle. A grown-up Boy Scout with a fine variety of scars for merit badges.

She smiled at him, just a little, then found herself unable to look away. Her smile dropped off by inches, lost and forgotten. They stared at one another while time slowed and pooled in the shadowed corners of the room. The air was thick with unspoken curiosity and soft, strange anticipation of...something almost within their grasp. Whatever happened would happen...but not tonight.

"It's been a long day," Billy said in an oddly strained voice. "I'll leave and let you get some rest. Is there anything else you need?"

Strange, Julie thought, still staring. Throughout her privileged life, she had always felt something terribly vital was missing, something she needed but couldn't find, buy or borrow. But now, standing face-to-face with a man she had known for only two days, she realized the nagging, empty space inside her was mysteriously sated. "No, thank you. I have everything I need tonight."

He nodded, changing his weight from one foot to another, reluctant to actually walk out the door. When he did that, he wouldn't see her again for hours. "You're sure? Maybe some warm milk or something? Except I doubt Colin has any milk in the refrigerator. I could check—"

"I gave up warm milk when I was four years old. But thank you, anyway."

"Okay, then. Fine." He cleared his throat, exasperated with his own asinine behavior. It wasn't like him. "I suppose I could read you your rights, but since I'm not arresting you, that would be silly. Before I make a bigger fool of myself, I'll wish you sweet—"

"Get your hands up, now! Don't breathe, don't turn around. Get your hands up!"

This from a third person in the room, and Billy Lucas, undercover cop of great renown, hadn't heard a damn thing. Instinctively, he crouched and went for the gun that was no longer there. Also acting on instinct, Julie screamed, whirled towards the door and screamed again. At the same time, mindful of her instructions, she reached for the ceiling.

There was a man standing in the doorway pointing a gun at them. In his other hand, he held a beer can.

"Don't be stupid," said the new, quite deadly voice, watching Billy's movements from behind. "I just had this place carpeted, and I'll be really ticked off if your blood stains it. Get your damn hands up."

Billy started to do as he was told, then froze. "Colin?"

"Lucas?"

Julie's head was swinging from one man to the other so quickly, she was dizzy. The blond, spiky-haired intruder looked downright disappointed, lowering his gun and lifting his beer to his lips. "Damn it, I thought I was going to have some fun. What a shame."

Billy turned on his heel, looking ready to kill the best friend he had in the world. "What the hell are you doing here? You're never here. Do you know you almost *shot* me?"

The light-haired fellow took a long swallow of beer, green eyes changing from menace to merriment in a split second. "Did not. You're the one who actually shoots people, I just threaten them." His curious gaze roamed over Julie head to toe and toe to head. What he saw seemed to please him mightily. "Still, maybe I should have shot you after all, Lucas. Who is your beautiful friend?"

"Can I put my hands down?" Julie asked faintly.

Colin nodded. "Sure thing. Sorry about that."

Julie tottered over to the bed and sat on the edge. Her mind told her this was Colin, and the threat of imminent death was simply a case of mistaken identity. Her emotions, however, had a hard time shrugging it off. Did these people actually live like this, skipping along the fine line between life and death with such blithe assurance? *Zap,* in the blink of an eye Colin was nice and normal not two seconds after he threatened to kill them.

This never happened in Palm Beach.

"I've never had a gun pointed at me," she said shakily. "I need a bit of time to adjust before I meet you, Colin. Please forgive my manners."

"She's a purebred!" Colin said gleefully. "You never cease to amaze me, Lucas." Then, to Julie, "How do you do? I'm Colin Spears, and I'm your new friend. I'm sorry about the gun, really. Usually I don't need guns with women."

Billy's blood went from simmer to boil when Colin started flirting with Julie. "Stop it right there," he said through gritted teeth. "She's off-limits, pal. Got it?"

"Yes, Billy," Colin replied meekly, green eyes dancing a tango. "I'm sorry, Billy. I thought you were an intruder, Billy."

"So what's with the beer?" Billy yelled. "You're trying to tell me you thought an intruder was up here, but you stopped at the fridge for a beer?"

"Yes." He took another swig. "I was thirsty."

Billy knelt down on the carpet in front of Julie. "This jerk is Colin Spears, and I'm going to beat him black and blue after you go to sleep. Are you all right?"

"Fine," Julie said dazedly. Then, a new light in her eyes, "it was sort of a rush."

"A purebred with spirit!" Colin whooped. "I'm going to shoot you after all, Lucas. I want her for myself. Where did you get that ugly-as-sin car in the garage? It looks like a little lime."

Billy knew he was in dangerous water at this point. Colin was half-looped, which wasn't unusual when he was off-duty, but he tended to talk too much when he was well-oiled. If he happened to say anything contrary to Billy's "vacation" story, Billy would be in deep trouble. Any reference to Billy's new security firm or recent retirement from the force would be highly unwelcome under the circumstances. "You're very tired," he told Julie. "I'm going to get Colin out of here so you can get some rest."

"But it's his house. We can't stay here now. We need to find a motel, Billy."

"No, we don't," Billy replied, giving Colin a look that clearly said *behave*. "Colin is only staying for one night. He never stays in one place more than one night at a time."

"Really?" Despite the threatening look Billy gave him, Colin's voice dripped with exaggerated disappointment. "I thought I came up for a week. I must have been mistaken."

"That's right," Billy muttered, his anxious gaze still roaming over Julie's pale features. "You were mistaken, Colin. I'll let you know just how mistaken when we go downstairs. Julie, get some sleep. I'm sorry about this incredibly unwelcome visitor."

"Like she said, it's my house," Colin whined, the gun still dangling from his fingers. "What do you mean visitor?"

"Shut up, Colin. Drink your beer." To Julie, "We'll sort it out in the morning, all right? If you need me, I'll be right downstairs."

"So will I!" Colin piped in.

"How reassuring," Julie murmured, her glazed eyes still focused on Colin's gun. "You should...you might want to put that away now. I just discovered I don't like guns."

"Oh." Colin slipped his gun back in the waistband of his jeans. "Sorry."

"Good night, Julie." Billy wanted to say more, do more for her, but Colin had to be eliminated from the equation, the room, and hopefully the condo, as quickly as possible. Raking a hand through his hair, Billy got to his feet and headed for the doorway. "You'll be coming downstairs now, Spears."

"Figured as much." Colin wiggled his fingers at Julie. "Nighty-night, beautiful angel in my bed. Tomorrow we'll do lunch, just the two of us."

"The hell you will." Billy grabbed Colin by the arm, dragging him along with tightly muscled force. Billy was bigger than Colin, angrier than Colin and far more experienced when it came to manhandling reluctant companions. Bearing this in mind, Colin toddled along like a good boy.

"Parting is such sweet sorrow," he called out to Julie, bright-eyed and full of good humor, despite the fact he was being hauled off like a petty criminal. "That I shall say...I shall say...Lucas, what's the rest of it?"

"Shut up, Colin."

Colin shook his head. "No, you fool. That's not it. Easy, you're spilling my—"

The door closed with audible force, cutting short Colin's recitation. Still wide-eyed, still short of breath, her heart still jumping like a rabbit in her chest, Julie flopped backwards on the bed.

Her adventure was taking on a startling life of its own.

"So you're still lying for a living?"

Slumped on the sofa with a beer in hand, Billy raised one eyebrow at Colin. He had spent as little time as possible explaining the Julie/Harris/Billy thing, hoping Colin wouldn't delve too deep. Just a job, he had told Colin. Nothing more. "You know what they say...old dog, new tricks, not a chance. So don't shoot your mouth off and blow this for me. I'm making a hell of a lot more money than I ever did risking my life."

"I should say," Colin murmured. "Seeing as how you're getting paid by both the brother *and* the angel. Nice going."

Billy grunted. It was the only sound he could trust himself to make. Colin knew the old Billy, the "pre-Julie" Billy. Naturally he figured Billy was still looking out for number one. If Billy protested too much—there was the Shakespeare thing again—Colin might see too much. From the beginning, Billy knew he had been something of a hero to Colin. Colin had come on the force when Billy was strutting the streets in his full glory, taking bullets and diving into battle with great enthusiasm. He had little to lose, therefore why not put it on the line whenever duty called? *We're all dying,* he'd been fond of saying. *Just some of us are doing it faster than others. Pass the pretzels and give me another beer.*

Unfortunately, the cynicism and "bad boy" attitude that made Billy such a legendary cop was translating into something less appealing as an ordinary citizen. He didn't want to be called upon to explain that to Colin, not right now when his heart and head were scrambled like a dozen broken eggs. He was still a guy's guy, he told himself. Still the hardy American mutt, doing just fine for himself without noble lineage or a drop of blue blood.

"You're such a moron," Colin replied idly, concentrating on opening the second beer of their reunion. "I meant you're lying to me, not the lady upstairs. Well, actually you're lying to all of us, but I know better."

The American mutt slumped further down in the sofa.

Here we go, he thought. I should have known Colin would see right through me. "I don't want to talk about Julie. You know the story. Leave it alone."

Some people would have been intimidated by Billy's dark look and flat tone. Unfortunately, Colin was not one of them. "No."

"Don't make me kill you," Billy said, only half in jest.

"I'd thought nothing could surprise me after working with the Wonder Undercover Boy in Oakland, but I was wrong. You, my oft-injured friend, have developed a conscience. Not only that—"

"You're cruising, pal."

"Will you stop with the threats? I'm the one with the gun in the room. Where was I?" Colin scratched his head for a minute, trying to think. "I hate this haircut, I really do. Oh, yes. Not only have you developed a conscience, but I see a glimmer of a heart, as well. She's gotten to you, hasn't she? I never thought I would see the day. Can you hear the sound of the hearts breaking all over southern California?"

"I've only known her for a couple of days."

Colin's eyes held a knowing gleam. "And how long have you been *watching* her?"

Billy sighed. This was the downside of having friends, true friends who didn't think twice before hitting you mercilessly with the unvarnished truth. Still, Colin had called his bluff, and unlike in their old poker games, Billy had lost. "I've been watching Julie Roper for three weeks, three days and about—" he consulted his watch "—six hours and twenty minutes."

"How the mighty have fallen." All traces of humor left Colin's face. He was younger than Billy, with absolutely no experience in the realm of selfless emotion, and no desire to rectify the situation. Still, he knew it when he saw it. "Lucas…no one thinks more of you than I do. I won't admit that again, so treasure the information. But you and I thrive in places someone like Julie Roper would drown in. We've got our strengths, and they keep us alive, but that's been bred into us. We keep guard over the rest of the world, we don't mingle with it. I know I just met Julie, but she has upper class written all over her beautiful face. High altitude, tip-top, cream of the crop, upper, *upper* class."

Billy put down his untouched beer, got to his feet and walked to the sliding glass door. Had he bothered to look beyond, he could have seen the peaceful white curl of the waves washing the shoreline far below. His mind, however, was stubbornly imprinted with Julie's delicate china-doll image. "I know," he said softly. "I've tried not to think about it, but I know what you're telling me. I'm all right with how this is going to end."

"Are you?"

He turned, giving Colin an oddly blank look. "I'm lying again, just in case you don't know."

"Oh, I know. I also know that none of this is really any of my business, so feel free to belt me and put an end to the discussion."

"You're too easy a mark. Where's the challenge in knocking out a little guy with a crew cut?"

Colin looked pained at the mention of his recent loss. "I feel naked, Lucas, and not the good kind of naked. With God as my witness, I swear I will never be without my ponytail again."

Billy smiled faintly, more than happy to change the subject. "As long as you're wearing blue and handing out speeding tickets, you're doomed to the clean-cut look. And while we're talking about your bad luck, you'll have to make yourself scarce for the rest of the week. I'll spring for a hotel.''

"This is *so* not fair," Colin grumbled. "I've been sitting in that damn trial for weeks, dreaming about getting down here and having some fun. We won, by the way. The guy got life."

"I'm happy for you. But not happy enough to let you stay here and hit on Julie."

"I have to be honest with you—that's exactly what I would do." Colin sighed and tossed his empty beer can across the room, a perfect slam-dunk into the trash can. "I feel so unwanted. Can I at least sleep with you on the pull-out bed?"

"Hell, no. But I'll take the floor since I'm appropriating your house."

A wide smile split Colin's face. "Okay. This is just like old times. Remember the stakeout on Downington Street? Thirteen days and nights with warm beer, cold pizza and a hard floor. Oh man, those were the days. Don't you miss the craziness sometimes? Don't you get bored and want to take a bullet or something?"

"At first I missed the excitement," Billy admitted, his eyes taking on a faraway look. "But lately, it's been all right. Lately it's been…good."

"Lately," Colin concluded flatly. "As in the past three weeks, three days, six hours and twenty minutes?"

"Yeah."

Colin shook his head sadly, mourning now for a new, more unexpected loss. "This is horrible. You did take a bullet, my friend. This time in the vicinity of the heart."

"I'll survive," Billy said. "I always do, don't I?"

Because of his sincere concern for his friend, Colin risked one last cautionary observation. "She's not from your planet, Lucas. In her world, they wouldn't have a clue who you were, and they wouldn't much like it when they found out. What do they know about survivors?''

"They?''

"The privileged class,'' Colin replied. "In case you haven't figured it out, we belong to another group a little further on down the food chain. Myself, I wouldn't have it any other way. That's the secret to being happy, my friend—being content with your lot in life. Plus, we get to carry a gun, which is also cool.''

"Have I ever told you how much I appreciate your advice?''

Colin looked pleased. "No.''

"Good.''

Seven

And so it had come to this.

Julie Roper of the Palm Beach Ropers was wearing men's slacks, a white Fruit of the Loom T-shirt and, incredibly, a pair of nicely bleached men's briefs. The entire outfit was securely fastened with a skinny black tie she had found in Colin's closet. Rummaging in Colin's drawers for something to wear had been terribly rude but quite necessary. She hoped he wouldn't mind. The Gator Getaway outfit was badly in need of a wash, and Julie was badly in need of clothes and makeup. She decided vacation wish number one would be to buy a few things off the rack. Wish number two would take her to a thrift store for a few necessities. She'd never been to a thrift store, so here would be another new experience to add to her growing list.

From the moment she opened her eyes that morning, she was in a "champagne" mood, feeling golden and

tickled from the inside out. The startling events of the
night before had taken on a luster of their own as Julie
relived Colin's thrilling arrival. She decided no life was
complete without having heard of those four thrilling
words: Get your hands up.

It just kept getting better and better.

She had seen a new side of Billy when Colin had ar-
rived, a terribly appealing macho thing she found fascinating. Neither Harris nor Beau had ever struck her as
being particularly blessed with raw masculine charisma,
but the instinctive, good-natured rivalry Colin and Billy
shared positively dripped with earthy magnetism. Like
every other aspect of Billy's emerging character, she
found his camaraderie with another male fascinating. Billy
was a man's man through and through. And although
Colin had been quite pleasant after he decided not to shoot
them, Billy possessed an aura of supreme experience and
self-confidence that overshadowed the younger man's
boyish appeal. Someday, if Colin was very, very lucky,
he might grow up to be as macho as his best friend.

Her hair was still wet from her shower when she carefully descended the stairs, hands holding up the hem of
her slacks just as she would hold up the skirt of an evening gown. The aroma of coffee filled the air, and California sunshine dropped a welcoming, hazy square of
white on the carpet—but no Billy. She poured herself a
cup of coffee, then wandered out to the balcony to check
the beach for her bodyguard. No Billy, no Colin, no any-
body.

When she heard a raspy, muffler-type rumble coming
from the garage, she smiled, set her coffee on the table
and headed for the second set of stairs. Oh, she loved
surprises. These days life was handing her one right after
another.

The garage door was open, and in the daylight she could see a testosterone vision in a black leather vest, denim shirt and stone-washed jeans sitting astride a huge motorcycle. She didn't know which was more impressive, Billy's aura of road-warrior wildness, or the gleaming, hungry-sounding machine. He sat astride the beast with lazy confidence, looking like a long-haired James Dean anxious to hit the road.

"The car is gone," Julie said while she shamelessly salivated.

"Colin wanted to borrow it. We traded transportation for a couple of days." He grinned, white teeth flashing in his tanned face. "Good morning, boss. Nice outfit, but the pants look a little precarious."

Julie lifted her T-shirt just high enough to show off her new belt. "I'm secure. I hope Colin won't mind."

"He won't know," Billy replied. "He had an over-whelming urge to drive a lime-green rental car and sight-see up and down the coast. We won't see him for a couple of days if we're lucky."

"I can't hear you over the motorcycle," she said. "Colin wanted to what?"

"Never mind Colin." He revved the motorcycle delib-erately, his reckless smile rearranging the rhythm of her heartbeat. "Wanna go for a ride, little girl? We can begin your vacation from convention in style."

Elated, Julie climbed on the bike behind Billy. She nearly melted the plastic soles of her shoes on the exhaust pipe before Billy explained to her where her feet went. He dropped a helmet on her head and told her to hang on to him with all her might, mind and strength.

Julie had never ridden a motorcycle before. She had never held on to any man with all her might, mind and strength. She found both experiences wonderfully exhilarating. She loved the wild wind that went along for the ride, loved the feeling of being closer to the people and the cars and the flowering shrubs they passed at what seemed like lightspeed. The shapes and shades blurred into one another, like a Monet watercolor. She loved the rock-hard strength she felt in Billy's muscles, the tight ridges of bone and sinew. He was warm and confident and so very male, and those qualities were irresistible to a sheltered innocent. It felt as though the more trust she put in him, the more independence she gained. She recognized a sensation of power and passion rising within her, and she tightened her choke-hold on Billy's waist. *Mine, mine,* she thought fiercely, then had to grin at her own temerity. This uncharacteristic intensity was just one more surprise that came along with the hazy, jangly, laid-back ease of the California artists' colony. There were people everywhere on the streets, in everything from bicycles to mopeds to convertibles, crowding the intersections and sidewalk cafés. All the structures seemed to be made of either white or pink stucco, and they greedily crowded each other all the way from the sea to the tops of the foothills. So many people, and Julie Roper was just a face in the crowd. Just another tourist, but one who was truly having the most glorious time of her life.

They parked the bike, then strolled the downtown village area where no motorized vehicles were allowed. It was like being in the middle of a giant art festival, complete with Italian ices, sidewalk music and bright banners flying from storefronts. Julie's somewhat unusual attire earned her a few pitying looks, and she was quite sure if she'd held out a hat, she would have received several charitable contributions. Not a soul asked her where she had found her "divine outfit." In fact, she put off visiting any of the twenty or so clothing boutiques until they had walked the full length of the village and back again, ending up right where they had started.

"Last chance to buy something," Billy told her teasingly. "Or are you enthralled with Colin's wardrobe?"

"No, but I was so enthralled with the motorcycle, I forgot my purse."

"My treat."

"Not when it comes to clothes. I've been known to spend five hundred dollars on a pair of shoes." She pursed her lips and whistled, stretching her brown eyes wide. "My, oh my, just imagine what I could spend on an entire vacation wardrobe."

Billy lost a shade or two of color. It occurred to him that he should have taken her to a thrift store and told her it was one of the "ordinary experiences" she'd been so hungry for. "Really? You've actually bought shoes that cost five hundred dollars? All right, let me rephrase my offer. Let's not go for an entire vacation wardrobe all at once. Do you think you could buy what you need for the cost of, say, *one* designer shoe?"

"A challenge!" Julie laughed up at him teasingly, luxuriating in the day, the weather, the surroundings and, last but definitely not least, the man beside her. She had no intention of allowing Billy to spend his own hard-earned money on her clothes, but she would allow him to make her a short-term loan. How amazing...she had a budget! Most of the people of her acquaintance would describe this day as nothing special, but for Julie, it was extraordinary. "All right, you're on. I can be very creative when it comes to fashion."

The store they visited was almost identical to the other clothing stores in the village: stuffed from front to back with bright fabrics, Hawaiian sundresses, T-shirts, baseball caps and swimsuits. Everything but the swimsuits was made of cotton and incredibly affordable. Julie hadn't done much buying "off the rack," but she'd always been very good at visualizing shapes, colors and cuts. This talent had earned her a spot on the Best Dressed List of Palm Beach, but she'd always given credit to Versace, Calvin Klein and Vera Wang. Today she would enjoy the experience of being dressed by Julie Roper.

Billy sat in a neon-pink overstuffed chair near the dressing room. He was the only male in the place, which bothered him. He was sitting on something pink, which bothered him. On the plus side, he had a very good view of Julie's feet beneath the dressing-room door. He grinned when she kicked off her plastic shoes and he saw that her toes were tipped with vivid silver polish. He watched as Colin's pants, tie and T-shirt hit the floor in a heap. His imagination kicked into high gear at that point and he forced himself to study the brilliantly colored kite hanging from the ceiling of the store. It was a Chinese dragon, sporting a long tail of orange and red cellophane. That is a very realistic dragon, Billy thought, fiercely trying to distract himself from the goings-on in the dressing room. Very colorful. Fine workmanship.

It didn't work.

"Do I get to see?" he asked.

From behind the louvered door: "See what?"

"You. I mean, the clothes. I have a very good eye."

"You have two very nice eyes." Julie walked out of the dressing room and did a quick twirl, giving him a whimsical, slightly embarrassed smile. She experienced an odd tightness in her chest as his hooded gaze drank her in. She was wearing a black halter swimsuit topped with a low-riding wrap-around scarf serving as a skirt. It was all quite modest, yet there was something in Billy's expression that made her acutely self-conscious. "What?

You don't like it? The whole outfit costs less than thirty dollars. Thirty dollars! It's absolutely amazing what bargains there are here. Yes? No?''

Billy was struck mute. He was mesmerized, capturing her image in his mind, wanting to hold it there always and forever. Her body was slight, yet generously curved. Her legs were long and shapely beneath the thigh-high scarf, gleaming with a golden tan. Her waist was impossibly small, her breasts lovingly outlined in the stretchy black suit. The very, very tight stretchy black suit. The shimmery, very, very tight stretchy black suit. Blond hair flew every which way, yet the expert cut left her looking intentionally disheveled. And her eyes...they were drenched with curiosity, bashful doubt and a shadow of sensual awareness.

"Looks like it fits okay," he managed hoarsely.

Julie looked disappointed. "It fits? You don't like it, do you?"

"I didn't say that." Billy had never sat outside a dressing room before while a woman tried on clothes. He didn't know the rules. "Isn't that the point, to find stuff that fits?"

"You hate it." She frowned, turning back to the dressing room. "Never mind. I have lots more to show you."

Billy took a deep breath, thinking how much he would like to follow her back into the dressing room. Instead, all he could do was look at her cute little polished toes and lust after them. He'd always appreciated the company of women, but he'd never stepped over the line into obsession, or even fascination. With Julie, he'd not only crossed the line, he'd hit it at a dead run, leapt over it and kept on going like the Energizer Bunny. He had no idea what came after obscssion, but whatever it was, he was heading straight for it.

She continued modeling for him. He broke out into a sweat and shrugged off the leather vest he wore. He saw her in a parade of strappy little sundresses, tank tops and skirts, shorts and bright summer-print shirts. Nothing was particularly revealing; there was no reason in the world he should be in acute physical discomfort that worsened every time she walked out of that damned little room. Finally he got to his feet, needing to put distance between himself and Julie. "I'm going outside for a smoke," he said.

Julie poked her head out of the dressing room door, frowning. "I've never seen you smoke."

"I don't," he told her. Her shoulders were bare, he noticed with an inner whimper of pain. Which probably meant the rest of her was bare, as well. *What does not kill us makes us stronger.* "But I've always liked to try new things. Give me a shout when they tally everything up."

When they left the shop, Julie carried a large shopping bag that held two sundresses, khaki slacks, tan shorts, a couple of T-shirts, a pair of jeans and a short, stone-washed denim skirt. She'd also purchased a swimsuit that Billy hadn't seen her model. It was quite different from the others she'd tried on, rather sinfully different. It was a glowing shade of buttery yellow, which contrasted beautifully with her golden tan. It was also a two-piece strapless bikini, which violated every rule Harris had ever set forth concerning modest and appropriate attire for young women. She had no idea if she would ever wear it, but she knew darn well if Billy saw her in it, he would be thinking something quite different from how well it fit.

The person who had happily purchased this rather flimsy wardrobe was not Julie Roper. Julie Roper wasn't in the habit of buying clothing that hadn't been measured to fit, then delivered to her home. She also didn't wear plastic beaded earrings strung on something that appeared to be dental floss, which she had purchased at the boutique. Buy one pair, get one free. Now, what savvy shopper could turn that down? This stranger inhabiting her body was spontaneous, easy to please and perfectly happy wearing dental floss dangling from her ears. No one judged her here; she was simply another tourist enjoying the lovely California sunshine.

"I wonder what my name is?" she mused aloud, strolling side by side with Billy.

He cocked one eyebrow at her. "You don't know your name?"

"Haven't the foggiest idea." She shook her head, enjoying the feeling of the long earrings dancing against her cheeks. "It's not Julie Roper, that's for sure. I'm much more interesting than Julie Roper ever was."

"That's hard to believe."

"Oh, it's true. I always knew how my days were planned weeks in advance. I never had any choices to make, and life is very dull when you have no choices. The person I am right now, however, has a *world* of choices right in front of her. I could go skinny-dipping in the middle of the night. I could dye my hair. I could get a tattoo—"

"What?"

"—and we could buy Rollerblades and skate all over Laguna. Oh, I just thought of something else! I could learn to drive Colin's motorcycle!"

"*What?*"

"And we could buy hot dogs and marshmallows and have a weenie roast on the beach. I've never done that. Isn't that a sad thing? When I told you I had a wish list, those were the kinds of things I was talking about. Normal, everyday things that no one in my social circle would ever dream of doing. I'd like to try surfing. And bowling! I've *always* wanted to try bowling.''

"Bowling?" whimpered the battle-scarred veteran of the streets. "What about my reputation?"

"And pool! Harris says playing pool is a pastime for the working class, but I think it looks fun. And you know what else I'd like to do? I'd like to learn to cook. I've never really prepared a meal by myself. Oh Billy, I could go on forever. I feel like I've lived in this world for well over twenty years, and I don't know it at all.'' She stopped in the parking lot beside the motorcycle, looking up at Billy with earnest brown eyes. "Do you know what the temperature of a dead body is?"

Billy was starting to feel dizzy and disoriented, as if someone had shot him. "A dead body?"

"Well, it's seventy-two degrees. Coincidentally, our homes in Miami and California are thermostatically controlled to remain at seventy-two degrees at all times. The same with every car we own. Regardless of the weather, everything stays at seventy-two degrees. Just lately I realized I have a lot in common with a dead body. I don't want to be comfortable any longer. I want to go beyond my comfort zone.''

"What does Bo-Bo do for your comfort zone?" Billy heard himself ask. He hadn't intended to take the conversation in that direction, but he didn't seem to have a lot of willpower these days. "Is he able to raise the temperature of your comfort zone?"

Julie looked away, feeling the hot sting of blood in her face. "This isn't about Beau. It's about me. I need to know who I am before I can figure out what I want."

"And you have how long before you become engaged?" Billy persisted, feeling suddenly irritable. "The sixteenth? That doesn't leave you much time to find yourself, does it?''

''I didn't say I was getting engaged on my birthday.'' Pouting, Julie stuffed her package into the roomy storage bin on the rear of the motorcycle. ''I don't know what I'm going to do on my birthday. I'm only going to worry about today.''

''Whatever.'' Billy climbed on the bike, waiting as Julie wiggled her way on behind him. To have her this close, to feel her hips molding against him, was an exquisite torture. He glanced down at her clasped hands holding so tightly to his waist. He looked at her bare ring finger. He tried to envision what sort of engagement ring Bo-Bo would choose. Enormous, more than likely. The sheer weight of it would probably give Julie carpal tunnel syndrome. What an inconsiderate jerk that Bo-Bo was. Were it up to Billy, he would chose something delicate, a ring that wouldn't overpower her small, delicate fingers...or his small, delicate bank account.

And why the hell was he even thinking such things? In less than a week, this little fairy tale would be over for both of them. Julie would wing her way home and take her rightful place in the world of the Palm Beach elite. It was where she belonged, what she had been born to. He had no place in that world. And she was only visiting his world, enjoying the novelty of an ''ordinary'' life. It would wear off. Novelties always did.

Another thought occurred to him. Was he a novelty, as well?

''We're not going anywhere,'' Julie pointed out from behind him.

Tonelessly, ''I realize that.''

''I'm starving,'' she urged. ''How about going to a diner? You know, the kind of restaurant that serves meat loaf and greasy fries and big, thick, gooey chocolate milk shakes. Is there a place like that around here?"

Billy started up the motorcycle. "You said it yourself, princess. Anything you want, you can find in California."

The diner experience was overrated.

For all her enthusiasm, Julie's tastebuds were accustomed to gourmet meals. Her stomach simply didn't know what to do with a generous serving of lard-drenched french fries.

"I think I'm full," she said, forcing herself to swallow the second of what appeared to be thousands of french fries on her plate. She had also managed a small bite of an equally greasy hamburger. "Diner food goes a long way, doesn't it?"

Billy smiled without much humor. "I guess this place isn't as great as I remembered. Would you like to order something else? Maybe a salad?"

She shook her head. "No, I'm fine. This place is kind of funky, actually. It has a very realistic sixties look, with the vinyl booths and Formica tables. Retro is very in right now."

"The diner is realistic because it's been here since the sixties. Original vinyl booths—hence the split seams—and original Formica tables. Lucky for them, retro is very in right now."

"You're making fun of me."

"Actually I think I'm making fun of me." Billy stared at her for the longest time, not moving, not saying a word. Had Julie been able to read his mind, she would have been astounded by his silent chant: *She's going to break my heart, she's going to break my heart, she's going to break my heart....*

"What on earth are you thinking?" Julie asked, puzzled at the strange expression on his face. "You've been awfully quiet since we got here."

"I was working on my cheeseburger," Billy said. Which was partly true. Cops didn't worry about eating well on their salaries. They worried about eating.

"And what about the rest of the time?" Julie fidgeted in her chair but managed to hold on to his unrelenting gaze. "You keep staring at me. You're doing it right now."

Why, indeed? Probably because he knew he had come to the end of his self-control. It came to him just like that, the knowledge that his reservoir of discipline was dry as dust. Heaven help them both.

"I'm *with* you," Billy said distractedly. "It makes sense to look at you, don't you think? If I stared at that lady sitting in the booth by the door, she'd think I was coming on to her."

"Why on earth would she think that?"

"Listen carefully." His heart be damned, he was going for it. He leaned forward, blue eyes growing ever darker and deeper. His expression was deadly serious, his fingers threaded tightly on the tabletop. His hooded gaze had never been more intense, or more unguarded. "If I looked at her the way I'm looking at you, she'd know exactly what I'm feeling. She'd see the need, the want, the uncertainty and the fear." A pause. Then, so softly she could barely hear, "Can't you see what you do to me?"

It was all so blunt, so unexpected, it took Julie a stunned moment to absorb it. Oh yes, she could see it all in his eyes, every feeling he had. Just like that, as if he had perfected some way of choosing whether or not to reveal himself to the world. No doubt his job had taught him how to operate on automatic pilot, what to show and what to hide. And now, for whatever reason, he had deliberately chosen to let her see inside him. He was vulnerable now, just as she was.

"Why tell me now?" she whispered, touching shaking fingers to her lips.

"Now is all I have," Billy replied, a brief flicker of pain in his eyes.

"Now is all any of us have, Billy." He seemed very alone to her suddenly, isolated in his scarred doubt. Her own eyes glistened with pent-up emotions, highlighting her thoughts and fears. He read her as he had been reading her all along.

"Have I scared you?" he asked, desire and apprehension swirling through his hot blood.

"A little." With a misty smile she stood up, holding out her hand to him. "And I like it. Let's go home, Billy."

Billy was the absolute best at many things: target practice, defensive driving, making spaghetti, ironing his dress blues, giving interviews without giving anything away and healing quickly from assorted wounds. He was not an unaccomplished man, but he was less than experienced when it came to building a bonfire on the beach.

"You didn't tell me it was your first bonfire, too," Julie shouted, fanning her face to keep the blasting heat from setting her hair on fire. She had to shout; the delightful crackle of an open fire had grown into a thundering roar within seconds.

"I think I shouldn't have doused it with gasoline," Billy said. "Not a gallon of it, anyway."

"What?"

"The gasoline made it…never mind. Let us flee for our lives." He took her hand and ran due north of the fire, heading for an outcrop of mossy green rocks. There he had spread the quilt from Colin's bed and placed a cooler full of food. "Until that inferno burns down, we're going to hide."

"Why?" Not that Julie minded. She wanted to be close to him. It was all she had thought about since leaving the diner: everything that lay ahead. They had gone shopping for marshmallows and hot dogs, exchanging hot looks and eloquent sighs as they walked up and down the aisles. Purchasing lowly hot dogs had never been so erotic. Home again, she had changed into one of her new outfits, tan shorts and a scoop-neck navy tank top. She knew she looked good because when Billy saw her, he couldn't say a word for a full minute. She was learning more and more about him. When his emotions were close to the surface, the teasing banter stopped and a taut silence took over. He'd walked very slowly across the room, took her hand and pressed a single kiss in the center of her palm. The palm, Julie discovered, was a very sensual part of the body.

They settled themselves on the blanket side by side before Billy answered. "The thing of it is," he said cheerfully, "it's illegal to have a fire on the beach here. I figured we could get away with it if we kept it small, but I fear the entire Laguna fire department could very well show up at any second."

"But you're a policeman," Julie pointed out. "Doesn't that give you a few extra privileges?"

"Not when you're burning down half the town just to roast a hot dog." His smile fell off. Her innocent statement reminded him of the lies that still stood between them. He'd been trying to forget, to give himself a few precious hours of pretending the winds of fate were finally whispering in his favor. Was it too much to ask, that for once he had something clean and pure and precious? Julie was something beyond his realm of experience. Everything in his life until he'd met her had been soiled, compromised and unpleasantly realistic. Julie was the polar opposite of everything he'd ever known and everyone he had ever met.

Julie looked at the ocean waves curling softly against the sand, slowly creeping inland. "At least we have plenty of water to put the fire out. You have to look at the positive side of things."

Billy stared at her beautiful profile, at the half-moon shadows her thick lashes cast against her delicate skin. The fading sunset cast a hazy rainbow of violet and rose over her porcelain complexion, giving her an ethereal, otherworldly look. Again, he thought of angels. "You've taught me that."

She looked at him, her eyes stretched wide in surprise. "I've taught you something?"

"Is that so impossible?"

She grinned, thinking back to her ineptitude when it came to pumping gas. "Highly unlikely. I don't get out much, you know."

An odd quiet fell between them, the same storm-tossed silence that had lingered with them since they'd left the diner. Julie shivered, though not from the cool evening breeze.

"Are you cold?" Billy asked immediately. "I could run back and grab you a sweatshirt."

Julie shook her head. "I'm not cold." She held his eyes, a shy smile tilting the corners of her wide mouth. "I'm trying to send you a message with ESP. I'm concentrating very, very hard. Can you hear me?"

For all her innocence, the message in her eyes was unmistakable. Billy swallowed over the knot in his throat, running a hand through his dark mane of hair. "Something about...the six damnable inches between us?"

"You're a regular psychic, Officer. What else?"

His gaze drifted to her beautiful, beautiful lips. "Something about my kissing you?"

"Wrong," Julie said softly.

"Wrong?" The poor man looked devastated.

"It was actually something about—" she rolled over to her side, eliminating the six damnable inches "—my kissing *you*."

And she did.

His lips felt so good to her, so familiar and welcoming. Her eyes fluttered closed as she savored the sensations coursing through her mind and body. She slanted her head this way and that, lightly exploring the softness of his mouth. Her tongue edged the corners, riding liquid fire in its wake. Softness and gentleness were replaced by a sweet deep hunger so quickly, her mouth parted with a fierce little gasp. In a clinical situation, it could be said she had reached the outer perimeters of her experience.

But Billy knew that, just as he seemed to know everything about her. He took over without missing a beat, rolling her onto her back, his hands pinning hers above her head. Still his mouth plundered hers, never sated, seeking more and more. As the length of his body settled perfectly over hers, a prickling heat fused their skin together. He began to ache, deep down inside. He felt her hips rocking ever so slightly with an age-old, primitive move. Arching. And this was just a kiss. Like the bonfire, it was all out of control almost before it began.

Julie's hands dug into his hair, loving the cold silk running over her fingers. The kiss was an exercise in contrasts, soft yet demanding, hard yet gentle. So many sensations all coming at once, driving every rational thought from her head. He created a need in her, and she truly thought she would die if it weren't filled.

The sand shifted beneath the movements of their bodies, creating a slight hollow like a well-worn bed. Julie's breath caught in her throat as Billy's hands slipped beneath her shirt, fingers splaying over warm skin.

"I didn't plan this...here..." He couldn't form the words between his kisses.

"I did." Like his, her hands had pulled the back of his shirt from his jeans, exploring the smooth stretch of skin with ardent hunger. Her fingertips touched a scar, ran along the puckered edges. Beneath him, her eyes took on a softness and wisdom he had never seen before.

"So many things could have taken you away from me. In the beginning I thought it was exciting, the life you lead. But now...when I think I might never have met you, when I realize what could have happened to you—"

"Don't." He kissed her gently on her forehead, his hands trembling on either side of her face. "We're here now. And having you appear in my sorry life is nothing short of a miracle."

"I'm the one who is lucky." She pushed his hair back from his forehead, smiling as it fell right back over his eyes. "You look like a little boy, Billy Lucas. Except for your eyes, and..." she blushed like a red, red rose "...and other things."

"Speaking of other things..." In all his life, Billy had never had so much trouble asking a simple question. Probably because he'd never held an angel in his arms before. "You've never been with anyone?"

"No." She wasn't embarrassed. In fact, on some subconscious level, she was supremely grateful there had been no one before him. It made the whole experience even more precious. "Just you, Billy. Only you."

It was a gift he had never been given before. He felt tears choke his throat, which absolutely no one from his former life would have believed. Billy was not a man of great emotional sensitivity, or so they believed. He was grateful everyone had been wrong about Billy Lucas, including himself.

"I would never want anything to hurt you," he said. "Are you...I need to know if you're..."

Her smile was that of a grown-up woman. His question in the heat of passion told her again just how much he cared. "Perfectly safe. I've been waiting to meet you since I was eighteen years old. I wasn't about to leave anything to chance."

Billy rested his forehead against hers, taking a long, hard breath. "The bonfire in a public place is illegal. Our personal fire in a public place is also illegal." Then he grinned, because he was Billy, and his sense of the absurd popped up at the most inopportune times. "I forgot about the weenie roast. How hungry are you?"

She assumed great solemnity, resisting the urge to drag his lips back to hers. "I'm very hungry, Billy."

"Really?"

"Now ask me what I'm hungry *for*."

"Oh, boy." Billy spent a hard thirty seconds considering the consequences of a private act in a public place. "For an angel, you have the most devilish mind. Will you walk me back to the condo? And up the stairs? And tuck me into bed?" *And make time stand still,* he thought silently.

"Yes, Billy," she whispered.

She'd been waiting to say that single little word all her life. Staring at Billy's tangle of dark hair above his crinkly blue-blue eyes, at the flush of his skin that made him look hot and golden to her, she knew the wait had been well worth it.

It wasn't his first time, but it felt like it.

They stood face-to-face in the upstairs bedroom, the quiltless bed separating them by six feet. How had that happened? Billy wondered.

"Look how far away you are," Julie pointed out softly.

"I'm right where I should be. You're the one who went to the wrong side of the bed." *Oh, that was good, Lucas. Why don't you just tell her you're paralyzed with desire and ask for a little help? That ought to impress her.*

"Your voice is shaking," Julie whispered.

"So is yours."

She tilted her head to one side, that secret, Mona Lisa smile back on her face. "I'll meet you in the middle."

They both smiled, hanging on to one another's eyes like a lifeline. At almost the same time, they slowly climbed on the bed, crawling across the mattress on hands and knees until their mouths were within touching distance. Their kiss was soft and sweet, lingering long after it ended, like a particularly haunting song. The melody of love, Billy thought with uncharacteristic romanticism, was far different from the dull meter of meaningless passion.

It *was* his first time, after all.

Still on their knees, they rose up chest to chest. Julie's eyes were luminous as she stared at him, dazed with utter longing. He memorized her features with his mouth, kissing her forehead, her cheekbones, the tip of her nose and the softness of her chin. She sighed, hanging on to his shoulders for support. She had no backbone, no means of support for her wobbly limbs. Billy's head slipped to her neck, his mouth raining kisses from beneath her earlobe to the base of her throat where a rapid pulse hammered. His hands spanned her waist, fingers nearly touching.

"You're so small," he whispered against her skin, his breath coming as softly as a caress. "Fragile…"

"I'm not fragile," Julie gasped, feeling his hands moving upwards to the thrust of her breasts. They felt so heavy, weighted with desire. "I'm…I'm…Ohhh…"

He kissed her deeply, his thumbs brushing over suddenly hard nipples. The kiss went on and on, until they were both gasping for air.

Billy shook back his hair, the surface of his skin burning feverishly. He needed to see her, to memorize everything about this moment. The expression on her beautiful face was like a sonnet, sweetly evocative and utterly captivating. Tumbled hair, swollen lips, angel eyes. What had he ever done to deserve this woman?

He reached for the hem of her tank top, slowly lifting it up over her head. Julie cooperated like a child being undressed for bed, holding her arms high above her head. The tank top went sailing, landing on the dresser. Still she held his eyes, watching his features as he stared at her white lace bra that left nothing to the imagination. His hands slipped behind her back, fumbling for a long minute.

"I'm trembling," he explained hoarsely. "I can't get the—"

With a shaky smile, she reached behind, unhooked the bra and sent it flying after the tank top. A slight flush of embarrassment sheened her skin, but the desire in her eyes remained hot and burning. Billy opened his mouth to say something, then decided to put it to better use. His kisses trailed from her throat to her breasts, giving devoted attention to first one, then the other. Julie was completely unprepared for the rush of pure sensuality that shuddered through her. Her head fell weakly back on her neck and her eyes drifted half-closed. Heaven. This had to be heaven.

But there was so much more. They kissed with broken gasps, hands searching and discovering. Billy shrugged out of his shirt with fierce impatience, wanting to feel skin against skin. Naked from the waist up, they came together for the first time. Her breasts flattened hard against his muscled chest, the most intimate connection she had ever had with another human being. Unashamed, excited, greedy…she felt so much, wanted answers to her half-formed thoughts and questions. She *wanted.*

They fell backwards on the bed without breaking the contact of their lips. Billy's weight was hard and thrilling over the restless movements of her hips. Her knee shifted between his legs, touching him *there,* trying to find new ways to get closer to him. Every movement she made, every gasp, every inexperienced touch, incited him to a deeper arousal. Fingers fumbled at waistbands, wanting to be closer still. The second coming together of naked skin was powerfully seductive, a flame that fed on itself. Now there was nothing between them, nothing but warm air, explosive need and a simmering dampness on their flushed bodies.

Billy had magic. He knew all the secrets of her body better than Julie knew them herself. His hands were gentle and seeking, knowing where and how to touch her. His lips carried kisses to places that made her whimper with unexpected pleasure. Billy had magic that lifted her up on a powerful wind, magic that left her there hovering until she thought she would go mad. Everything in her body was arched, urging, straining. And when Billy entered her, she went even higher, floating on a mindless plain of desire. She'd heard stories of what poor virgins endured—

clinical tales of the birds and the bees designed by Harris to put the fear of God in her. Messy business, he'd said, blushing so hard, she expected steam to come from his ears. For procreation, not recreation. And vastly—ahem— overrated.

Harris had lied.

When Billy began moving within her, Julie's hands dug into his shoulders, and she bit her lips as her head twisted from side to side on the pillow. She was quickly frantic from the growing intensity of the age-old rhythm. This was a new universe of sensuality, filled with hot sparklers and swirling clouds of glitter. She tried to keep her eyes locked with his, mesmerized by the emotions she saw in his face. He was wild-eyed, tense and hungry. His eyes, his hands, his body made claim on her in every way he knew how.

Mindless, shivering, she began moving with him. She was utterly deaf to the anguished pleas she made, but Billy heard and answered them all: "Please…yes…give me…"

It was all he could do to wait until she reached her summit, watching with fierce pleasure as her eyes opened wide and her breathing broke in jagged, gasping pieces. Beneath him, her angel face took on the luminous shimmer of pearls, enhancing her femininity and beauty to a level that stunned him. She was a revelation to him, delicate and womanly in every sense. She was a miracle. *His* miracle.

"I'm so grateful for you," he whispered, the words breaking over the tight emotion in his throat. Had the little sound he made lived to grow up, it might have been a sob.

When the blessed relief came for him, it was both a death and a rebirth, agonizing in its pleasure. Billy had never known such volatile passion could be tempered with such soul-searing tenderness. He could hardly see her through the sparkling moisture gathering in his eyes. Not tears, because Billy had never cried in his life, and certainly not because of an unbearable happiness.

Not tears, he thought, his shaking hands framing her lovely face. *Big boys don't cry.*

A single drop trailed down his cheek, wetting the hot skin at the base of Julie's throat like a subtle, intimate baptism. He closed his eyes until he had himself under control, then looked at her again, bright fever spots burning on his cheeks. He had finally found it, the elusive, never-before-attained feeling of completion. He was in awe of her.

"It's never been like this before," he said hoarsely. "I didn't know. You are...the world to me. A world I've never seen before."

She pulled his head to her breast and held him with exquisite gentleness. "Billy," she whispered, tenderly smoothing his hair. On her lips, his name sounded like a prayer.

"What?"

"Just Billy."

Eight

Julie couldn't sleep, because she had something very important to do.

She had to look at Billy.

She sat cross-legged on the end of the bed, staring at the man sleeping so soundly smack-dab in the middle of the mattress. The sheets were so tangled and wrinkled, it looked as through they'd fought a whirlwind and lost. Billy's hair was likewise a victim of the wild wind, boyishly tousled around his sleep-flushed face. His cheeks were crinkled from the pillow, dusted with the beginnings of a dark beard. He slept folded up on his side like a baby, mouth parted and one fist curled on the pillow beside his head. With the rose-colored sunrise gilding his smooth brown skin, he looked much younger than his years.

But he was no boy.

Julie was wearing one of Colin's large white T-shirts

and nothing else. It had more to do with being a bit chilled than with modesty. Last night she had learned many new things about herself. She was remarkably *un*-modest in the right situation. Her enthusiasm had more than made up for her lack of knowledge. Billy had told her so a number of times throughout the night.

"Wish number one," she said very softly, smiling at the man who controlled the rhythm of her heart.

"I heard that," he said quite clearly.

"Of course you didn't. You're asleep."

He grinned, eyes still closed. In a proud little sing-song: "I'm wish number one..."

"You're full of yourself this morning, Officer. Maybe I wasn't looking at you when I said it."

"You were." He opened his eyes and turned over on his back, looping his arms around his neck. His thick-lashed eyes were still weighted with sleep, but sparkling with bright blue humor and supreme confidence. "I *know* these things. I was trained to be very observant. And right now I am observing you wearing one of Colin's white undershirts. I don't like your skin so close to Colin's undershirt. Come here and I'll take it off for you."

"I was cold," Julie explained.

"That's because you're way, way down there at the edge of the bed." He gave her his pirate's smile, wide and reckless. "Come here and I promise to warm you up in three seconds flat. Think of it as an official strip search."

Julie's beautiful smile slowly uncurled, and she stretched out her legs to lie down beside him. Unfortunately, there were certain places on her body that were rather tender this morning. She couldn't help but wince and bite her lip.

"What?" Billy said immediately, sitting bolt upright.

"Nothing. A little sensitivity comes along with becoming a woman, that's all."

Billy slapped his forehead with no little force. "What an idiot I am. I'm so sorry. I'll take care of you, sweetheart."

"You *did* take care of me." Her angelic smile turned slightly devilish. "You took care of me *sooo* good. Wait a minute…where are you going?"

Billy was on the move now, fueled by guilt, tenderness and protective sympathy. He jumped out of bed, giving her only a brief glimpse of his well-muscled body before pulling on his jeans. "I should be shot for being so insensitive. I'll go start you a bath. Colin has this great Jacuzzi that should be very soothing for…any parts that need soothing."

He headed off to the bathroom. Julie made a grab for the belt loop on his jeans, but missed. "Hold on, Romeo. This is the morning after. You can't just jump out of bed and tell me to take a bath. It's too abrupt. I'll have separation anxiety if you leave me alone in the Jacuzzi."

At this, Billy turned on his heel, giving her a slow-growing smile that melted her bones and turned her blood to honey. "Who said I was leaving you in there alone?"

At breakfast, she sat at the bar with a pillow between her bottom and the wooden stool. This time she was wearing Colin's bathrobe.

"How's your…granola?" Billy asked, looking anxiously at the pillow.

"My *granola* is doing just fine," Julie replied with a giggle. "Will you quit obsessing about me?"

"Never," he said simply. "And I'm sorry about the Jacuzzi, love. We're supposed to be giving you a rest, and what do I do? Can I get you another pillow?"

"Not unless you want my head to hit the ceiling. Will you stop? If you'll remember, I didn't want to get out of the Jacuzzi. That was your doing."

"We were becoming prunes." Billy scooted his bar stool as close to her as he could get. He was wearing nothing but low-slung jeans and a smile. Even his feet were bare, toes curling happily around the lowest rung of the stool. His long hair was still damp from the bath, sticking out a bit over his ears and down his neck. His shoulders were wide and powerful, every inch defined by lovely ridges of muscles and sinew. The smile lines that etched his eyes seemed deeper this morning, lending him an aura of sweetness and charm. His hard edges were softened, the cynical amusement gone. Happiness looked terribly good on him.

It was all Julie could do not to throw herself at him. Again.

"We should take a nap after breakfast," she suggested hopefully.

Billy nixed this with a shake of his head. "We're going to do something less...*strenuous* than napping. You need to be pampered, darn it."

"What could be less strenuous than a little nap?" she replied innocently.

"Running a marathon." He tried to look stern, but it was hard to keep a straight face. Julie had been a remarkable student, and after a certain point, she had even become a teacher. She had no fear of needing, no taste for games. Never had he felt so caught up in something so helplessly and devastatingly provocative. In her innocence, Julie gave without restraint, gave with all her body and soul. And the more she gave, the more he wanted.

Though it was not wise or in keeping with his duty as a gentleman, he found his gaze locked on her lips. They were reddened and slightly swollen, like a late-summer rose in full bloom. His pulse picked up.

"Then what would you like to do today?" she asked.

"Wish list," he managed, strain in his voice. "Yours, not mine. At the moment, mine is R-rated. You're on vacation, remember? You have all of sunny California at your feet, angel. Just tell me where you'd like to go."

Grinning, she pointed at the ceiling, indicating the upstairs bedroom.

"No," Billy said firmly, while his eyes unconsciously wooed her. "Although I'd like nothing better. We must distract ourselves." Then he offered the ultimate sacrifice. "Would you like to go bowling today?"

"Bowling?"

"It was on your wish list, wasn't it? And it's my duty to see each and every wish is fulfilled. Go upstairs and put on your bowling clothes."

"I don't—*hic*—have bowling—*hic*—clothes," Julie managed through a sudden case of hiccups. "Don't make me laugh. I get the hiccups every—*hic*—time I laugh. Gosh darn it."

"That is so incredibly cute." He looked at her with soft adoration, loving the way she stretched her eyes wide open and bounced on the bar stool every time she hiccuped. He was feeling so many things all at once, he could hardly identify one emotion from another. Still, the sum of it all was crystal-clear. Julie was the reason he would take each and every breath from this day on. Who would have thought an emotion as powerful as love could sneak up on him like this? The only thing that had managed to sneak up on Billy Lucas up to this point in his life had been a case of the measles. He was too damn good at protecting himself.

Stunned, he played back his thoughts and realized he had finally said the word, if only to himself. Love?

Love.

"So what do people wear when they go—*hic*—bowling?" she asked.

"Do you have a skirt, something fairly short?"

"Yes."

"Don't wear it. I will be watching you from behind, as will probably every other male in the bowling alley. Bear that in mind."

"Okay."

"Julie?" He stared down at his bowl of cereal, feeling terribly inadequate and inexperienced when it came to expressing his emotions. He settled for humor, mainly because he didn't want to scare her. Or himself. "Since you put an arrow straight through my heart last night, it's only fair that I beat you at bowling. Don't you agree?"

She smiled, her eyes luminous. She could see how new this was to him, and nothing could have made her happier. He had no more experience with affairs of the heart than she did. Who would have guessed? "Are you telling me you want me to throw the game?"

"You won't need to, love. You've never bowled before. My point was, I'm not going to be a gentleman and let you win."

"Ha! Wanna—*hic*—bet?"

She beat him. Badly.

Billy threw eight gutter balls in a row. On his last two attempts, he managed to knock down two pins. He was competing with a terribly unfair disadvantage. When it wasn't his turn, he had no choice but to watch Julie. He was worked up into a lather before she threw her second ball. She had no technique, no experience and did a great deal of grunting and groaning, but she still managed to knock down the pins. Holding the bowling ball like a watermelon, she approached the line in an awkward shuffle, dropped the ball with a thud and hopped up and down in excitement while she watched it roll. It went left, it went right, it went every which way except into the gutter. And when, by some sort of divine intervention, she actually got a strike, she whooped and hollered like a wild woman, drawing every eye in the place. She had hiccups nearly the entire time.

With customary male assurance, Billy decided it wasn't his fault he had lost. Staring at the south end of Julie's northbound body was an exercise in painful masochism. She was wearing the most stunning, adorable, mouth-watering pair of jeans he had ever seen in his life. Armani or Avanti or whatever his name was couldn't have improved upon the fit. The soft denim followed the stunning, adorable, luscious curves of her bottom with loving attention to detail, particularly around the rear-pocket area. And that was only when she was walking away from him. When she walked towards him, he was exposed to the most stunning powder-blue knit top that dipped just low enough to reveal the slight burgeoning curves of her breasts. Her body was beautifully proportioned and her "bowling clothes" made no secret of the fact. He watched her fiercely, all too conscious of his trip-hammering pulse. His game suffered.

Since he lost, he had to spring for lunch as their bet had stipulated. Julie chose to expose her Palm Beach tastebuds to Mexican fast food. This proved an excellent choice, far more enjoyable than the diner experience. Julie was instantly addicted to their Big Burrito Bonanza Meal. She polished off two entire orders by herself, which included burritos, potato fries and cherry empanadas.

"But you're so little," Billy said, watching her finish off the last of her potato fries with amazement. "Where is it all going?"

"I need my strength," Julie said, munching away contentedly. "Do you want the last of your taco?"

"Feel free. Are there any more like you back in Palm Beach?"

"Like me? What do you mean?"

"The ladies of your social circle. I have this vision of anorexic, well-preserved and self-conscious ladies who do lunch but never eat. You have ketchup on your chin."

Unfazed, Julie swiped at her chin with a napkin. "Obviously we're not all that way, or I wouldn't be sitting here making a pig of myself. I guess if I had to characterize most of my friends with one word, it would probably be relentlessly bored." She made short work of her last potato nugget. "That's two words, isn't it? Anyway, you get the idea. I don't remember much about my parents, but it seems to me they were pretty happy. My father was always laughing, always picking me up and twirling me around in the air. And my mother...she was truly the most beautiful woman I've ever seen. She was full of light, her eyes, her smile, her hair. I do remember that."

"What happened to them?" Billy asked, painfully aware he already knew and feeling like a louse.

"They were killed in a sailing accident when I was seven years old. I wish I could remember more about them, but at least the memories I do have are good ones. What about your parents?"

"Gone, too," he said shortly. "My mother died a few years ago from cancer. She was a strong lady, a fighter till the end. And my father...he never...he wasn't..." Then, abruptly, "He's gone, too."

"I'm so sorry," Julie said softly. "What happened to him?"

Billy opened his mouth to change the subject, make a joke, anything but tell her the truth about him. He was truly astonished when he heard himself tell her the truth. "There's no need for pity. I was only two years old when he left, so I don't even have a face to put to him. From what my mother told me, he was a heavy drinker with a short fuse. She never married again after that, so I imagine the experience was less than wonderful for her. Whenever anyone asks about him, I just tell them he's dead. He might be. Who knows?"

The sudden silence was jarring to Billy. He was painfully conscious that his heart was cracked wide open and bleeding in public. For whatever reason, Billy had always felt somehow responsible for his father's desertion. Immediately, he was sorry he had told her the truth.

Until he looked into her eyes. He saw no pity. He saw other emotions—empathy, understanding and regret for the boy Billy had been. Julie might be an innocent, but she had a great deal of experience in loss. And when it came right down to it, that was precisely what had happened to both of them: one way or another, they had lost the emotional security of two loving parents. They each had scars, some more visible than others.

"Who would have thought," Julie ventured thoughtfully, "that two such different people could have so much in common? Life is so unpredictable. Just when you figure you've got a handle on it, something new happens."

"At least you're not relentlessly bored."

"Heavens, no. I used to be, but that was B.B."

"B.B.?"

She grinned. "Before Billy. Then fate brought you to me on a dark road in the middle of a cypress swamp. I've been anything but bored since we met, Billy Lucas. I've been anything but unhappy, I've been anything but dissatisfied. Amen to the dissatisfied part.''

Billy's eyes lost a bit of their sparkle. Still, aware his precious time with her was limited, he slammed the door on his whimpering conscience. "Thank you. I try.''

She smiled at him, fluttering her eyelashes with exaggerated flirtatiousness. "While we're on the subject, what are the chances I could talk you into going home and taking a nap?''

"A nap," Billy said slowly, "or a *nap?*''

Julie yawned. "What on earth do you mean? I didn't get a lot of sleep last night. I just exhausted myself beating you at bowling. I need to sleep.''

"Oh.'' Billy's face fell comically. "Okay. Of course.''

"Billy?'' She kissed him on his cheek, then put her lips next to his ear and whispered, "Take me home so I can ravish you.''

Her lips brushing his ear tickled. Her words more than tickled. "Are you sure? You don't need…you know, a rest?''

"Resting is relentlessly boring. I gave that up, remember?''

"Amen.''

Life continued to be anything but boring.

Colin was waiting when they returned to the condo, slumped on the sofa, both legs propped up on the coffee table. He was eating a giant-size candy bar.

"Where have you two been?'' he complained. "I've been waiting all morning. Do you know there is a convention of Shriners in town? I'm not kidding. There isn't a room to be had in fifty square miles.''

"So try a hundred square miles," Billy said crossly.

He'd been very much looking forward to his "nap." In fact, they had actually managed a thirty-second make-out session on the motorcycle while stopped for a red light. Julie had claimed it was one of her wishes, and a damned fine wish it was. "You promised you would go away."

"I saw them come into town this morning," Colin went on, completely ignoring Billy's comment. "They're all on motorcycles, I swear to you, *motorcycles*. Every single one, and they all wear these funny little hats you wouldn't believe. The kind of hat an organ-grinder's monkey would wear. Anyway, my point is, they are giving motorcycles a bad name. They need to get themselves some Shriners' leather jackets."

"Hello, Colin," Julie said, amused despite the lingering sexual buzz thrumming through her body. She had never enjoyed a red light so much. "How are you?"

Colin wiggled his chocolate-stained fingers at her. "Hello, polite and beautiful woman. I'm just dandy, thank you. And you, Billy? Did you sleep well last night?"

"I wish I had my handcuffs," Billy said darkly.

"Let's have none of that kinky talk around here," Colin admonished. "There is a lady present. Where have you two been all morning?"

"Bowling," Julie said. "My very first time, and I won."

Colin blinked, his gaze swinging to Billy. "What?" he barked. "What? Lucas, you went bowling? Oh man, this is going to kill your reputation."

"If I pay you, will you go away?" Billy asked.

Colin's sunny smile gave his answer. He didn't need to say a word.

"If I pay you a lot?" Billy persisted.

"As amusing as the two of you are," Julie interrupted,

"I've got to visit the powder room. Besides, if this keeps up, I'll get the hiccups again. Excuse me."

After she left, Colin looked inquiringly at Billy. "Hiccups? Do devastatingly handsome men give her the hiccups?"

"Never mind what gives her the hiccups." Billy's keen gaze saw something in his best friend's expression Julie had not. There was a reason he was here, and judging from Colin's plastic smile, it was serious. "What's happened?"

"How do you know something's happened? Never mind, I forgot who I was talking to for a minute. The undercover psychic." Colin took a deep breath, looking down at his half-eaten candy bar. "Someone's looking for you, Lucas."

Oh boy, here it comes. Billy sank down on an overstuffed chair, his chin drooping to his chest. "Hell. Not now..."

"You knew it was bound to happen sooner or later," Colin replied quietly. "You told me as much last night, that you were living on borrowed time."

Billy closed his eyes, trying to steady himself. "I didn't know it would run out so fast."

"The captain paged me this morning. He'd had a visitor who asked about you. Claimed he was a detective hired by the beautiful lady's brother. He'd found out she had purchased tickets to California, and he was visiting your old haunts and talking to everyone who would talk to him. The captain didn't give him much information, but you know as well as I do it's only a matter of time before someone sends him down here. Everybody knows you spend a lot of time here. I'd say you have another twenty-four hours at best before he comes knocking."

So much for living in a dream. This was far worse than

Billy had imagined it would be, a million times worse. His throat was tight and burning, his stomach was tied in a hard knot and his clenched hands were white-knuckled. He had almost convinced himself his precious time with Julie would last forever. "I need to tell her before the walls come tumbling down."

"There's more," Colin went on reluctantly. "Harris Roper left a message for you with the captain in case he heard from you. He said to tell you he was going to press kidnaping charges if he didn't hear from you immediately. We both know it wouldn't stick, but the publicity would be huge, and that wouldn't do your new career any good. Call the guy."

"I don't give a damn about my career."

"That's what friends are for. Call. You've taken this thing as far as it can go, man."

Billy said a bad word and picked up the phone, keeping a wary eye on the stairs. Harris Roper answered on his private line halfway through the first ring.

"This better be you, Lucas," Harris snapped by way of greeting.

"It's me," Billy replied quietly. "I'm trying to get her home without letting her know you were having her watched. That's what you want, isn't it?"

"Home from where?" Harris demanded.

Billy hesitated. "California."

"I know that!" Harris barked. "Where in California?"

Billy's gaze was stark and expressionless. He looked up at Colin, who made a fierce threatening face. *Tell him,* Colin mouthed.

Billy opened his mouth and closed it again. Without consciously making the decision, he hung up on Harris Roper.

Colin's jaw was swinging as he gaped at the phone.

"What are you thinking? The guy can ruin you! You can't let your career go down the drain because you have a thing for Julie Roper."

A light of battle came into Billy's eyes. He himself was surprised at the sudden fury Colin's words inspired in him. "I haven't got a *thing* for her, Colin," he bit out. "It goes way beyond that."

There was a long silence. For once in his life, Colin seemed at a loss for something to say. Finally he stood up, looping his thumbs in the pockets of his jeans as he looked down at Billy. "Look man, I'm sorry. When I had to come back here today to tell you, I felt like death knocking at your door. Maybe I don't understand the way you feel about her. It's out of the realm of my shallow existence. But if you want a chance to salvage anything, you need to tell her the truth before her brother gives her an earful. Unless this private eye is a real moron, he'll find you. I mean, you could take off and go somewhere else, but that would just be postponing the inevitable. Not to mention the media frenzy if Harris Roper follows through with his threat. And from what I gather, he's got the money and the clout to do it."

"I know," Billy said dully. "I know."

"What do you know?" Julie asked cheerfully as she descended the stairs. "Are you guys leaving me out of something exciting?"

"Nope." Like a chameleon, Colin turned on his sunny charm to distract her attention from Billy's ravaged expression. "I was just saying goodbye. I've decided to go and join the Shriners. I must have one of those hats."

"It would cover up that crew cut you don't like," Julie replied teasingly.

"So would a wig, which I am also seriously considering. Well, folks, I'm outta here. I'm giving you your little rental car back, by the way. That car stinks. I'd rather drive a minivan, I swear.'' He gave Billy a speaking look. "So...I'll talk to you later, Lucas?''

"Yeah, later.'' Like the professional he was, Billy re-arranged his expression into something almost normal. "Thanks for...dropping by.''

"Why not stay for dinner?'' Julie offered, puzzled at the ever-so-subtle change of mood in the room. Both men looked quite normal, but she sensed something had con-spired between them. "Colin, if you want to stay here, Billy and I could go somewhere else. It would be no trou-ble at all. I don't want to cause any problems for you.''

Colin smiled, meeting her at the bottom of the stairs and gallantly kissing her hand. "Thank you, but I hear the Shriners calling my name. I wish you both all the best. I think it is absolutely wonderful that Billy has himself a girlfriend who says 'powder room' instead of 'john.' Class *and* looks in the same beautiful package. Good luck to both of you. Keep in touch, Lucas. Adieu.''

Colin's sudden absence felt like the startling peace in the eye of a hurricane. Julie shook her head and laughed, then promptly climbed up on Billy's lap and gave him a smacking kiss. "Hello, you. Your friend is funny.''

"Hello, you.'' Billy kissed her back, long and hard. When he broke from that kiss, Julie was gasping. "Do I take your breath away? I want to. Your breath, your soul, your body...I want it all.''

Julie stared at him, her head tilted slightly. "What's wrong?''

"Nothing.'' His forced smile felt tight against his cheeks. "Maybe I just want you to understand that I would do anything to be with you. All I want is to hold you...to know you'll stay here with me in this moment forever. Can I have that, or is it asking too much?''

"Not as far as I'm concerned." Julie still couldn't rid herself of the feeling she had missed something important. "Are you sure Colin wasn't angry that we're putting him out of his own house? He seemed...I don't know, upset about something."

"Colin's fine. He just wanted to get his motorcycle back. He's been called back to work unexpectedly, so he wouldn't be able to stay here, anyway." It was a good lie, delivered with the ease of many years of experience. Never show what you're thinking, never give anything away. Billy savaged himself inside to deaden his conscience. He realized he had just made a potentially dangerous decision.

He wasn't going to tell her, not yet. He wanted just a few more precious hours of pretending he was actually the person Julie believed him to be, a few more hours to cling to the idea he was someone who deserved to see the light of adoration in her eyes. Everything would change after that; the bubble would burst, and she would see the mangy American mutt for what he was—a liar, an opportunist and a fraud. He'd known all along he was living in a fool's paradise, but he'd never dreamed it would hurt so badly to face reality. Taking a few bullets was nothing compared to this. All this he told himself while smiling at his love as if tomorrow would bring nothing but happiness. Desperation was an amazing source of strength.

"So I don't need to feel so guilty because he left?" she replied teasingly.

"You don't need to feel guilty at all." *I have guilt enough for both of us.*

Softly, with a low throb of passion, "Good. Because what I'm feeling right now is a world away from guilt." She dipped her face to his, rubbing noses. "Ask me what I'm feeling, Officer."

"I can see what you're feeling," Billy said, his voice matching hers in intensity. Her splendid dark eyes were heavy with erotic imaginings, her lovely lips parted as she traced the sculpted line of his mouth with the tip of her tongue. He held himself still as long as he could, then his mouth swooped over hers and plundered mercilessly. Julie met him kiss for kiss; almost instantly a searing sexual heat blazing between them. Billy was kissing her as if it were the last day of his life, taking and giving all he could with fierce intensity. His hands moved with the same hunger, pulling at her clothes, wanting her skin against his. It didn't occur to him to be gentle or cautious. He only knew he had to have her. Now.

He moved them from the sofa to the floor, his foot kicking the coffee table out of the way. Neither of them noticed it tip over with a thud. Julie was groaning with pleasure against his mouth, her wide eyes glazed with recklessness. The sofa, the bed, the floor...it didn't matter. She had never known she was capable of such abandon, or such painful and instant need. She fed on him, on the breathtaking sexual hunger he radiated. She caught fire, rolling on the carpet in a tangle of intertwined limbs to escape their clothes. They were frenzied, hands and mouths everywhere, seeking satiation. Nothing existed at the moment beyond the ravaged aching of desire.

Once and only once did Billy pause in his lovemaking. His arms were outstretched on either side of Julie's shoulders, muscles damp and straining. His body was feverish, his mind filled with a terrible, wonderful mixture of love, passion and fear. The woman beneath him was trembling, her dark eyes nearly black with primeval sexual longing. Her cheeks were reddened from his light beard, her lips wet with sensual rain. Her breasts were crushed against his hard chest in soft surrender, her legs parted on either side of his. Her hectic breathing matched Billy's, harsh, rapid and shallow. There was nothing withheld, no hint of shyness or self-consciousness in her beautiful face.

She trusted him completely.

Billy's throat tightened painfully with the thought, then he fiercely pushed it away. He needed the solace of her body, he wanted to tell her without words what was happening with him. Words inevitably involved lies, and lies had no part in this moment. Julie received him joyously, matching his thrusts, urging him deeper still. This was something different than making love, Billy thought. He believed they had been creating love all along, from the first moment they had come face-to-face on a dark Florida road. No, this was an admission of their power over one another, a searing act of passion in its purest form. No one had ever felt like this before them, and no one ever would again. They knew exactly how rare and extraordinary this moment was.

Billy had been looking for a miracle and he'd found it, albeit only a temporary miracle. His thoughts expired in a wash of sensual release, purging guilt and fear. They found their solace together, deliberately lingering at the threshold of fulfillment for a timeless moment. She was his, and he had fiercely claimed every part of her, body and soul. Surrendering to that claim was the most satisfying experience of her life. Body to body, they dropped off that sheer cliff simultaneously, hearts stopping at the blinding rush of pleasure. The experience was so powerful, so overwhelming, they died and left the Earth together, then came back to it, reborn.

Nine

Later that afternoon, Julie curled up on the bed to "close her eyes for a moment." She slept for nearly an hour, during which time Billy walked on the beach. She knew because he was leaning against the frame of the doorway when she opened her eyes, bare feet sandy, hair tangled over his forehead and untucked white shirt sticking to his skin in damp patches. The knees of his jeans were dark and sandy as well, as if he'd been kneeling on the beach.

"Hello, man of my dreams," Julie said huskily, brown eyes beautifully drowsy. "You went off and left me."

"And you didn't even know it. Poor child, I tired you out." He walked slowly into the room, hands pushed deep in the pockets of his jeans. Although his lips were curved in a smile, there was something dark and unfamiliar in his eyes.

"What's happened?" Julie asked. "You seem... you're...different."

He ignored the question, sitting on the edge of the bed. "You look good in sheets. You should wear them more often."

"I plan to." Julie stretched, uncurling like a sleepy kitten. "I'm going to start a trend in Palm Beach. I did dream about you, you know."

He gave her a curious smile, head tilted to one side. "Did you? Tell me."

Julie sat up, the sheet drifting lower on the curve of her breasts. It didn't occur to her to pull it up again, either. She'd never felt safer, more uninhibited or more secure in her life. "It was a lovely replay of this afternoon downstairs. Just so you know, you were wonderful. Again."

"This afternoon," Billy repeated slowly, taking her small hand and slipping his fingers through hers. He stared at their clasped hands with great concentration. "I wasn't very gentle, was I? I've never been like that before. I surprise myself constantly when I'm with you. Are you sure it was a lovely replay and not a nightmare?"

Julie nodded solemnly, although her eyes were smiling. "Quite. Although looking at you makes me think I'm the one who should have been gentler." In a conspiratorial whisper: "You have a hickey on your neck."

He grinned, looking a bit more like the breezy, brash Billy she knew. "I know. That hasn't happened since high school. Did you know you can be arrested for giving an officer of the law a hickey?"

"Arrest me," Julie purred. "And then lock me in a tiny room with you and a few hot lights and question me. I promise it will be the very best interrogation you've ever had. I've never been interrogated before, but I'm showing a great deal of talent when it comes to running with the punches, don't you think?"

"That's rolling with the punches, cupcake."

"Rolling, running, whatever." She pulled up her legs, looping her arms over them and resting her chin on her knees. Her expression was whimsical. "Would you like to know a secret, Twinkie?"

"Twinkie?"

"You called me cupcake. I think Twinkie is a cute little pet name." She raised one finger when Billy opened his mouth to protest. "No, no, listen. I have to tell you something. It's terribly, extremely, *exceedingly* important."

His expression didn't change, but his eyes became opaque, unreadable. "I have to tell you something, too."

"Me first." She pursed her lips, blowing a tendril of sleep-mussed blond hair out of her eyes. "You know my famous wish list? All the things I've always wanted to do all my life, but never could?"

"How could I forget? Not many people have bowling on their wish lists for life."

"Well, I realized something today. We did it. We fulfilled every single wish I have ever had in my life. Not only do I feel completely satisfied—stop smirking, I don't mean that kind of satisfaction—well, I do, but..."

"You're rambling."

"Sometimes people are missing something, but they're not exactly sure what it is. That's what happened to me. Now I know I haven't been longing for freedom all my life. That was just the name I gave my loneliness. This whole adventure wasn't what I really wanted."

"Now she tells me."

"It was a *feeling* that was missing, Billy." Her brows drew together, her expression fiercely earnest. She wanted him to understand what an incredible change he had made in her life. "I've been so protected, I didn't know what it was like to experience life like everyone else. I've learned so much the past few days. Life is anything but a bore, and it's not something to be afraid of. It's absolutely glorious. It doesn't matter what you're doing—you could be a waitress or a ballerina or a zookeeper. The important thing is finding all the joy in every moment. Anticipation. Joy. Trust. If you feel those things, if you hold on to them, you don't need a wish list. That's what you've given me, Billy. The chance to be myself.''

Billy's mind was stuck on a single word: trust. His stomach felt sick, his emotions whirling in a dance of nauseating speed. He looked away from her, pretending to stare out the window. ''I didn't give you anything. You had it inside you all the time, Julie. You're not giving yourself enough credit.''

Julie hesitated, wondering at the odd tightness in his voice. She became conscious of a subtle tension in the room, a strange echoing sensation of emotions reverberating from wall to wall. ''What's wrong?'' she asked quietly, her eyes looking like big, dark wounds in her face. ''Something was wrong when you walked into the room, I saw it. Did I say something wrong?''

''No.'' It was all he could do to manage the single word. ''It's not you.''

She tried to smile. ''Billy, you're starting to scare me. I've got my heart in my hand here, if you haven't noticed.''

He took a deep breath, closing his eyes for a moment, trying to anchor himself inside to something, anything. Now was the time to tell her everything. Now.

''I love you,'' Julie whispered.

The world ground to a bone-snapping stop. Billy's eyes flew to hers like a rocket, bright blue and amazed. In a barely audible croak, ''What did you say?''

She swallowed hard, stunned at her own temerity. Where had that come from? She'd been falling in love with Billy Lucas from the beginning, but to actually admit it, just like that, bold as you please…well, it took her as much by surprise as it did Billy. She reached out a tremulous hand, gently touching the side of his face. "I'm sorry. Now you're the one who's scared. Just forget I said that."

"Forget?" Talk about having a wish list. This was more than Billy had ever hoped for, more than he had dared to let himself imagine. A woman like Julie Roper, who could have any man on the planet…

And she loved Billy Lucas, a man who had never considered himself particularly lovable.

"I didn't expect this," he whispered. "Not in a million years."

He saw instantly that he had said the wrong thing. Her face turned hot. She pulled the sheets up to her neck. "You know what they say…fools rush in. Sorry about that, Officer. Sometimes I just open my mouth to change feet. You know, I'm hungry. I'm starving. I could go for some lovely steak tartare, or shrimp scampi. That sounds wonderful. Let's go out to eat." Before Billy could stem the tidal wave of conversation, she was up and out of the bed, wrapping the sheet around her like a sari. Suddenly she had all her old inhibitions back. "I'm going to shower," she said, continuing with the brittle, rapid-fire pace of her speech. "It's a beautiful night, don't you think? What a shame it would be to spend it inside—"

"Julie—"

She pretended not to hear him, marching toward the bathroom. "Maybe a nice bath. I absolutely adore relaxing in a Jacuzzi."

Hells bells, she was starting to sound like a Palm Beach bunny again. All the walls were up, and Billy couldn't blame her. "Julie, if you'd just wait—"

She waved a hand dismissively. "We'll chat later. I won't be too long. You might want to consider taking a quick shower yourself; you're covered with sand." A short but deafening pause here. "Downstairs."

Julie took refuge in the bathroom, slamming the door shut behind her, then leaning hard against it. She felt as if her body was a clumsy shell, completely disconnected from her mind. She was feverish, half-crazy with embarrassment and regret. It wasn't so much what Billy had said that had pushed her close to tears.

It was what he hadn't said.

Julie was utterly miserable throughout dinner, although nothing in her expression or tone of voice gave it away. She had been born and bred in Palm Beach, and that gave her an advantage when it came to flawless composure in social situations. She could pretend with the best of them.

Still, Billy knew. It was there in his eyes every time he looked at her, the reminder that somehow she had blundered terribly by telling him she loved him. It was between them like electric static, constantly threatening a painful shock if they got too close. He smiled, she smiled, the waiter came and went and the evening passed without one referral to anything even remotely personal. It was amazing how fast things could change.

The restaurant was only two blocks from the condominium, and since it was such a beautiful evening, Julie had suggested they walk. In truth, she simply couldn't face being ensconced with Billy in the small confines of the rental car. Once it had been comforting. Suddenly it was unbearable.

It was still early when they left the restaurant, the last gasp of a stunning violet sky bleeding into the ocean. Julie pointed out its beauty not once, not twice, but three times in as many minutes. And they still had a block and a half to go.

Billy had said little throughout dinner. He knew what she was thinking and why she was thinking it. And until he told her the entire unvarnished truth, he had no right to accept what she had offered him. In point of fact, he had had no right to consummate their relationship, but it was too late to change anything. In all his life, he had never wanted anything more than he wanted her love…or felt less deserving of it. He was damned if he told her, and damned if he didn't. It was a good word, he decided grimly, describing perfectly how he felt.

Damned.

He had known from the beginning he wasn't good enough for her. He hadn't the breeding, the class or the financial wherewithal to even consider himself worthy of someone like Julie. Not to mention the fact he was a liar and a fraud. He could hardly count the number of lies he had told her from their very first meeting. Initially it had been to protect her. Now it was to protect himself as well, to win just a little more time with her before reality came crashing down around him. In a perfect world, he would have been privileged and upstanding, a man like Bo-Bo who had been born into a good family with a shiny bright future. Billy had known a different world, a grimy and dangerous existence without prospects or promises. He had done what was necessary to survive and done it well. But he wasn't in Julie's class and never would be. She was light, he was dark. She was truth, he was deception.

Quietly, quickly and helplessly, he was going out of his mind. What happens when you meet the one person you can't live without, and you can't have her? No matter how long and hard he thought, he couldn't come up with a solution that would bridge the gap between them.

They were nearly at the condo when he saw the car. It was a limousine, long, white and shiny, idling in the driveway. The windows were tinted black, but he knew who was inside.

"Uh-oh," Julie said slowly, spotting the limo. Harris always used a limo when he was traveling. But there was no way he could have tracked them down. He didn't even know Billy, let alone Colin. Still…

"Does Colin ever use a limo?" she asked faintly, knowing the answer.

"No." His time was up, Billy realized. He grabbed her arm, his mind going a hundred miles an hour. "Wait. Just wait. You need to listen to me before you talk to your brother. I need to tell you…" His voice trailed off, his eyes anguished as they watched the limo driver get out of the car to open the passenger's door. "Damn…I'm so sorry, Julie."

"Sorry about what?" Julie was completely bewildered. Still, something in her heart winced, preparing for an unknown assault. Then, when Billy did nothing but stare at her, "Billy? You're scaring me. Say something."

He couldn't. He felt his stomach drop as Harris Roper climbed out of the limo. He looked almost fragile, suspenders hanging on to his little shoulders for dear life. But he carried a terrifying impact, a painful reality.

"It's your brother," Billy said dully. It was too late now. Maybe it had been too late from the very beginning. "I didn't think it would happen so soon."

"You knew he was coming?" Color drained out of Julie's face. She had the sickening sensation of something dark and unfriendly crawling up behind her. "You're not surprised," she whispered. "You knew…"

"I knew he was close. I wanted to tell you—"

"Julie!" Harris ran up to his sister, enfolding her in his

arms. "Are you all right? Do you have any idea what you put me through? Why on earth—"

"Don't." Julie pushed Harris away, looking at Billy over her brother's shoulder. "Don't ask any questions, Harris. Just answer a few."

"You're angry?" Harris looked astonished. "I'm the one who's been searching all over the country for you and our friend Billy here."

"How did you know his name?" she asked. Her lips felt numb, as if she were slowly freezing to death. "I told you I hired security, but I never told you his name."

Still Billy said nothing. The brief, brilliant happiness he had known was flying further away on a wild, cold wind. Harris looked at him, his eyes accusing. "What the hell is she talking about? Are you telling me you allowed her to hire you? Where are your morals, your principles? You were already working for me! You can be certain you won't be collecting your money, I'll tell you that much, mister. From either of us."

"I don't want your damned money," Billy said. He couldn't take his eyes off Julie, nor she him. Her expressions were clear and honest, as usual. Fear. Confusion. Devastation. And every emotion was a very personal gift from Billy Lucas. "I couldn't tell you," he said.

Julie needed to sit down. It didn't matter that she was standing on the curb in front of the condo. She dropped to her knees on the grass, her hands folded tightly in the billowing skirt of her sundress. She closed her eyes briefly, trying to stem the nausea she felt. "Harris? How did you know his name?"

"I told you. I hired him as security several weeks ago." Harris paused, clearing his throat. "Julie, you can't just sit there on the grass. We can talk inside, all right? I can explain everything."

"I'm sure you can," she replied. "So explain right now."

After an awkward moment, Harris hitched up his beige slacks and gingerly sat down next to his sister. "I can't imagine why we must discuss this sitting on the ground. But if we must…Julie, I was worried about you. When you have as much money as we do, you can't be too careful. There are kidnapers and felons—"

"Kidnapers *are* felons," Billy said tonelessly.

Harris glared up at Billy. He clearly didn't relish the experience of sitting so far beneath him. "When I want your opinion, I'll ask for it."

"I can't wait." Billy's eyes were dark, the evening breeze playing with his long hair. "If you'd like me to go in the house—?"

"Stay here," Julie told him. Her voice was soft, but the expression on her face wasn't. "Harris?"

"You're making such a fuss about nothing," Harris replied. "Granted, I should have told you, but you never seem to take our position seriously. You needed a personal bodyguard, and I knew you wouldn't agree if I consulted you. Can we please go inside and talk? I've never been comfortable on grass."

Julie ignored his question. "So you hired Billy to watch me? When was that?"

"Four weeks ago," Harris admitted, looking embarrassed for the first time. "And it was working very well until he absconded with you. Needless to say, this man will never work for anyone again as a bodyguard. I already have my lawyers—"

"Shut up, Harris," Julie said, in no mood to be distracted from her questions. "How is it I never saw him?"

"Because I'm good," Billy told her flatly. He was feeling incredibly masochistic at this point. He deserved this, all of it.

She looked up at him, a silent and painful communication passing between them. "You're not a policeman, are you?"

"I was. I retired and started a security business. I was referred to your brother by a detective in Florida I'd worked with."

"And I'll get that disreputable excuse for a civil servant, as well!" Harris announced, one finger pointing up at Billy. "I'll have my lawyers on him so fast—"

"Shut up, Harris," Billy said, still staring at Julie. "I wanted to tell you. But I knew what would happen when I did. Not only would there be problems between you and your brother, but our time together would be over. I couldn't face that."

"Time together?" Harris sputtered. "Together? Good grief, what have you done, Julie? You have a personal relationship with your own kidnaper? Is that what you're trying to tell me?"

"I'm not telling you anything, Harris. I'm asking the questions." Her eyes felt blistered, her vision blurred. "And he is your employee, not my kidnaper. So you had him watching me for the past four weeks? Billy has been living at our home?"

"No, no, the chauffeur's apartment," Harris assured her. "I had several cameras installed so as to protect your privacy. I didn't want you to feel uncomfortable, and you always say the security people make you feel uncomfortable." He waited, perhaps hoping for some sort of thanks. It didn't come.

"So Billy has been watching me for all that time," she said to no one in particular. "Cameras. My own private bodyguard, watching me through hidden cameras...."

"I wanted to tell you," Billy said again. He felt like a broken record, soon to be thrown out in the trash. "I'm so sorry. I don't know what else to say."

"Are you expensive?" she asked, her voice brittle.

Billy closed his eyes briefly. "Very. I told you, I came highly recommended."

"And I told you, there will be legal repercussions!" Harris blustered. "Your reputation will be sorely—"

"Shut up, Harris," Billy and Julie said in unison. Julie got to her feet, hoping she had enough strength to walk the few yards to the car. Anger was a great motivator, even when your heart had stopped beating some time ago. Harris quickly followed suit, brushing his slacks for any lingering debris.

"We'll go now," he announced, obviously relieved to have some distance between himself and the grass. "We need to put this entire unfortunate experience behind us as quickly as possible. I'm sure you'll agree."

"It doesn't matter if I agree or not," Julie said icily. "My feelings are of no importance to either one of you, or this wouldn't have happened. Did you really think you were in the right, Harris? That your concern for me excused the deception?"

Harris looked surprised, then acutely uncomfortable. "Well...that really isn't the issue here. My trust was betrayed by someone I hired to give me peace of mind. I had your best interests at heart, Julie, you know that. I always have. Now, getting back to your relationship with Lucas here, please tell me you're not—"

"That's none of your business, Harris." Julie's throat was so dry and tight, it hurt to speak. She turned her wounded gaze in Billy's direction. "You knew Harris was coming, didn't you? How?"

"Colin. That's why he came back this morning. He

wanted to tell me a detective your brother had hired was asking questions at my old precinct. It was common knowledge I spent a lot of time in Laguna, so it was only a matter of time until Harris showed up.''

''Another little conspiracy.'' She smiled without humor, her eyes still swimming in tears. ''You and Colin, you and Harris...I'm such a fool.''

''Who is Colin?'' Harris asked suspiciously, obviously wondering if there was yet another man he should be suing.

''Colin is no one.'' Though talking to Harris, Julie never broke eye contact with Billy. ''He doesn't matter to me any more than Billy does. I'm ready to go home, Harris. Now.''

''Your things?'' Harris asked. ''Don't you need to pack anything?''

''Nothing in that house is mine. It all belongs to someone else.''

''Someone *else?*'' Harris was starting to panic. ''Someone besides Colin and Billy? What on earth has been going on here?''

''Julie, wait.'' Billy watched her walk toward the limo with haunted eyes. This was every nightmare he had ever envisioned coming true. ''You're wrong if you think this was a job for me. Almost from the first moment—''

''Which first moment?'' Julie whirled on him, her hands clenched into tiny fists. ''The first moment you saw me through a camera or the first moment you saw me face-to-face? I'm just trying to get the story straight.''

Harris had never seen his sister so distraught. He ran an uncomfortable finger inside the collar of his white shirt. ''Julie, there's no need to upset yourself. It's over.''

''It never started,'' Julie said, all the anger and life suddenly draining out of her voice. ''Do you know what really bothers me, Billy? You had so many chances to tell me the truth. You knew what was happening between us. And you let it happen.''

"Dear heaven,'' Harris said faintly, his small shoulders slumping. ''Let what happen? What are we talking about here? Lucas, if you have in any way harmed my sister, I will—''

"Stop threatening people, Harris.'' Julie turned her accusing gaze on her brother. ''This is as much your fault as it is Billy's. You both lied to me, and you both did it for your own selfish reasons.''

"You're wrong,'' Billy told her, the crimson twilight sheening the anguish in his face like a wash of blood. ''What I felt...what I feel...is real. I knew when you discovered the truth it would all be over. Someone like you doesn't belong with someone like me. You are good and pure and unlike anyone I've ever known in my life. My only excuse is that I wanted every second I could have with you.''

"Because you knew it would end when I found out the truth.'' She shook her head, giving a strange, humorless laugh. ''You know something, Billy? I'm not leaving because we come from different worlds. What a ridiculous, soap-opera cop-out. Obviously you haven't a clue what love is, so I'll spell it out for you. I'm leaving because you didn't see the possibilities we had. You saw something temporary right from the beginning. I never even knew you, did I, Billy?''

"You knew me,'' Billy said quietly. ''I'm just a little disappointing.''

"Damn right you are.'' She turned away abruptly so he wouldn't see the hot tears spilling over her face. ''I need to get out of here. I need to leave.''

When Billy instinctively tried to stop her, Harris valiantly planted himself between them. "It's over, Lucas. You've done enough damage, don't you think?"

Billy looked Harris straight in the eyes, his anger flaring. "We both did quite a bit of damage. The difference is, you get to go home with her and try to earn her forgiveness. And if you're half the man I think you are, you'll back off and let her find her own life. She's more courageous and resourceful than either one of us give her credit for."

The intensity in Billy's voice took Harris by surprise. This was not the brash, supremely confident young warrior he had hired to secretly guard his sister. This was someone else altogether, a stranger racked with deep pain and guilt. His sincerity was unmistakable.

"You may be right," Harris told him, losing a bit of his bluster. "But it's no longer your concern. I'll send you your things. Dare I trust you not to try and contact her? To simply forget about her?"

Billy stared at him without a nuance of expression in his face. "I'll forget about her every day for the rest of my life, Harris. Don't worry. I know where I belong. And I know where she belongs."

Billy watched like a statue of stone as Harris and Julie disappeared inside the limo. Billy couldn't see through the black-tinted windows, but he knew she wasn't looking back at him as they drove away. She had too much pride and the hurt went far too deep.

Besides, there really wasn't much to look at.

Ten

Julie thought she was all cried out by the time they reached their home in Florida, but that lasted only until she wandered down to the chauffeur's apartment, against Harris's protests. She walked in the door and immediately watered up again.

It was amazing and terrible to think Billy Lucas had actually lived here for a full month before she had ever met him. The place seemed to be just as he had left it. There were clothes on the floor next to the bathroom, clothes on the bed, a watch and a pile of coins on the dresser. Discarded Popsicle wrappers were everywhere. Julie picked up a neon-orange T-shirt from the bed, holding it to her face and breathing deeply. She lost herself in the scent for the longest time, shoulders broken and shuddering under a fresh onslaught of tears.

Vision blurred, tears dripping off her chin, she looked

at the mound of pillows on the bed. She could still see the imprint of his head. She took a deep, sustaining breath and looked to the ceiling, literally wincing when she saw the cameras set up above the doorway.

"You shouldn't be down here," Harris said from the open doorway. "I think it would be a good idea if you slept up at the main house tonight."

Julie barely looked at him. "I don't feel like taking your advice right now, Harris."

"Julie, stop making this difficult." Harris sighed and walked into the apartment, giving the pile of dirty dishes a wide berth. "This place is a mess. I'll send the help down first thing in the morning."

"The help." Julie gave a short, humorless laugh. "Have you ever wondered why it is you and I can't get along in this life without 'help'? We have people to guard us, people to drive us, people to cook for us and people to clean up after us. Help, help, help."

"Of course we do." Harris stood on one leg, wrinkling his nose as he peeled a Popsicle wrapper off the sole of his shoe. "We're very—dear me, this doesn't want to come off—we're very fortunate."

"Then if you don't mind, I'm going to be *un*fortunate from now on." She sat down on the edge of the bed, unconsciously running her hand over the rumpled sheet. "As soon as I can arrange things, I'll be moving."

"That's ridiculous! Why move when we have twenty-nine bedrooms?"

She shook her head, her big, tired eyes seeming to swallow half her face. "*You* have twenty-nine bedrooms, Harris. You're the king of your castle. I don't know what I have or who I am, but I'm willing to take a chance and find out."

* * *

When Billy Lucas was happy, he ate banana Popsicles. When he was depressed, he ate popcorn laced with enough salt to give him a heart attack. There was popcorn in every room in the condo, popcorn on the sofa, popcorn on the deck, popcorn on the living-room carpet. The place smelled like a movie theater.

He told himself over and over he deserved the overwhelming guilt and grief he experienced each time he looked at the bed or the sofa or walked along the beach. He mourned as he had never mourned before. And, as with any full-blown depression, Billy stopped answering the phone after the first couple of days, realizing Julie wasn't going to call. He hadn't shaved in a week. He wore nothing but a pair of snug, low-riding jeans and a scowl. When he looked in the mirror, Tarzan looked back at him. He was running out of popcorn, and since his depression wasn't showing any sign of lifting, he knew he would have to leave his self-imposed exile and head for the market. He was trying to work up the energy to get off the sofa and go upstairs for a shirt when someone knocked at the front door.

His heart jumped and whirled in a triple somersault. He leapt off the couch like a deer in flight, racing toward the door. It wasn't Colin…he had a key. He could think of no one else who would come calling. Would she be there?

He opened the door and the triple somersault went *splat*.

It was Harris.

It was hard to say who looked the more depressed, the man inside the condo or the man standing on the front porch. Harris seemed even thinner than the last time Billy had seen him, shoulders stooped with weariness, hound-dog eyes big and dark with misery. He was wearing slacks and a dress shirt with a navy bow tie, but for once the suspenders were missing. His slacks were hanging perilously low on his narrow hips.

"We need to talk," Harris said, looking Billy up and down. "My word. Did you just get out of bed?"

"I haven't been to bed yet," Billy told him lifelessly. "And why would I want to talk to you? Last thing I heard, you were ready to hire a hit man to knock me off."

"I am a law-abiding citizen. I hire lawyers, not hit men." Ever the gentleman, he added, "I tried to call before I left Florida, but there was no answer. I was afraid you wouldn't be here."

Billy shaded his eyes against the intruding sunlight. "What do you want, Harris?"

"Can I come in?" Harris looked at him like a poor orphan begging for gruel. "Please?"

Billy shrugged, stepping back from the door. "Whatever."

Harris had never seen a popcorn depression before. He stopped short when he entered the living room, looking around with gaping astonishment. "Lucas? What happened here?"

"Julie happened," Billy snapped, heading for the bowl of popcorn on the table. "What can I do for you, Harris? Slit my throat? Jump off the balcony?"

"Of course not." Gingerly brushing the popcorn off the sofa, Harris sat down. His slight body seemed to vanish in the deep cushions. "This is very difficult for me."

"Sitting down?"

Harris folded his hands neatly in his lap. "Of course not. Asking you for assistance is very difficult, particularly when the last time I asked you for assistance you absconded with my sister. I have a situation at home."

"A situation?" Billy lifted one dark brow. "Is that the rich and privileged way of saying you have a problem?"

"Yes," Harris snapped. "It is. My sister will not do what I tell her. In point of fact, she has put her life in extreme danger. She doesn't know how to swim."

Billy stared at him. "You've lost me."

"She bought a houseboat moored in the Keys, just like that, sight unseen. A houseboat that floats on water. You cannot put security gates on water. She moved down there yesterday."

A ghost of a smile touched Billy's lips. "Good for her. Knowing Julie, she'll have one hell of an adventure." Then, hesitantly, "What about Bo-Bo?"

"Bo-Bo?" Harris took four pieces of popcorn out of the bowl, one at a time. "You mean Beauregard? They are only friends. She's made that perfectly clear."

There was a long pause. Billy's throat burned with the force of his frustration. "She'll get over it, Harris. I'm entirely forgettable. Don't lose any sleep over it."

"I must say, I thought your feelings for her went beyond this callous nonchalance."

"Why the hell can't you talk like everybody else?" Billy snapped. He practically threw the bowl of popcorn on the coffee table. "Nobody says *nonchalance*."

"Lucas, Julie has been an entirely different person since she left you last week. I know my sister better than anyone else in the world. Unless I miss my guess, she cares deeply about you."

"You missed your guess," Billy muttered. "She hates my guts."

"Nobody I know says *guts*," Harris retorted. "Do you love her?"

Billy groaned and slapped himself on the forehead. "Of course I love her! The whole world would love her if they had a chance. That changes nothing. She deserves better than me, Harris. You probably have more money in your pocket than I do in the bank. My father was a drunk, and I have no idea if he's dead or alive. I've been intimately acquainted with the darkest and most twisted souls you can imagine. I'm riddled with bullet holes, for hell's sake! Do you want to hear more?''

"No, that's enough," Harris replied mildly. He stood up, took a piece of paper out of his pocket and dropped it on the coffee table. "I've written down directions to her new floating house. Before I leave, I want to make something clear. Julie and I are fortunate enough to have financial security, but inheriting money is no test of worth. Julie is incredible because she is Julie. There have been times when I wished we hadn't been saddled with a fortune, so that I'd know whoever married her would be marrying her because of love. I encouraged Beau because he had a great deal more money than we did, so I didn't have to worry about his motives. I'm not a snob, Lucas. You, however, are. You refuse to fight for her because she has more money than you. How idiotic. If I weighed more than one hundred and twenty pounds, I do believe I would take a swing at you."

"You're forgetting something," Billy grated out. "She never wants to see me again."

"I imagine a woman in love is capable of forgiveness." Harris walked to the front door as cool as a little cucumber. "It's up to you now. You can't blame me if there's not a happy ending to this story. Or your father, your career, your bank balance. This time you'll have no one to blame but yourself."

The door closed between them, neatly and quietly. Billy remained on the sofa, shell-shocked. He let out a deep, tired breath, dropping his face in his hands. He was hurting so badly, it was difficult to think. Julie had been right when she'd accused him of seeing their relationship as only temporary. Believing in something permanent would have gone against everything he'd ever learned in his life. Having nothing left to lose was so comfortable.

The wind was picking up outside, rattling the sliding doors in their tracks. Drawn to the sound and fury of the coming storm, he wandered out to the balcony, hands shoved deep in the pockets of his jeans. Particles of sand hit his bare chest with a barrage of tiny stings he barely noticed. Hell, it felt so alien to him, this being *alone*. Ironic, considering the comfort he had always found in his own company. Then along came Julie, and Billy Lucas had learned how to need. The longing was so strong, always there, always pulling at him. After all this time, he had finally learned what real loneliness was.

He closed his eyes against the wind, trying to anchor himself to something solid in his soul. All he found was Julie, in his mind and his heart. How could he go day after day without her? Try as he might, he could find no strength in his convictions. He had told himself over and over he was doing the right thing for her. Why, then, did it feel so wrong?

And where did he go from here?

Eleven

It was not necessarily a bad thing to live alone.

In fact, it had been three weeks of great discovery for Julie. Peaceful and calm, an existence untroubled by bodyguards and interfering brothers and other lower life-forms. She loved her new home, though it was a far cry from her old home. There were no manicured gardens, no security gates standing between her and the ocean. For the first time in her life, she felt as if she was a part of the rest of the world. Her boat was moored in a shallow inlet along with a couple of ancient fishing boats. *Her* little home, no one else's. She told herself she had everything she needed to be happy. And she almost believed herself.

Julie doubted if she would ever live on dry land again. Her new "neighborhood" was a world away from the power lunches, jazzy nightclubs and general tourist infestation of Palm Beach. She loved the way her little houseboat lulled her to sleep every night with the soft rhythm of the waves, loved the gentle cricket sounds that filled the darkness and the brisk wake-up call of cool, morning sea air. There was a little town not far from the dock, a distance of less than a mile. She loved the name—Mystic Harbor. She went there to buy fruits and vegetables almost every day, enjoying the quiet stroll through the sleepy waterfront village.

She kept busy. She had her own meals to prepare. She bought her first bucket and mop and learned to scrub decks, collecting many slivers along the way. When her thoughts wandered to Billy and became unbearably painful, she cleaned. Her houseboat was worthy of the Good Houseboat-keeping Seal of Approval.

She wore a succession of tank tops and shorts, never bothering with makeup. Her hair was usually twisted up in a ponytail, and the polish on her bare toes had long since worn off. Her nails were chipped and badly in need of a manicure, which she had no intention of getting. As her mind and body began to relax, she realized the healing power of long afternoons spent lazing in the sun like a cat. She felt like a child of nature, a solitary mermaid living neither on land nor in the water.

Harris visited her twice, which was once too often. She was still angry with him, though she had stopped fearing he would take away her independence. He couldn't do that any longer, she was too strong, too determined. No one could. She served Harris tuna on toast, which he politely ate, then promptly lost. The subtle rocking motion of the houseboat did not agree with him. He made her promise to take swimming lessons, if only for his peace of mind. Then he made her cross her heart and promise again.

As far as Julie was concerned, her creaky, lemon-scented houseboat was the perfect haven for healing. She felt almost invisible there, just another little soul living out her days on God's green and blue Earth. She knew there would come a time when she would need more, a time to decide where to take her life from here. She thought about possible careers, but she was in no hurry.

There were times, usually at night, when she caught herself yearning for a man's touch, for the warmth of a male body next to hers. And not just any man; ironically, she ached for the man who had betrayed her and hurt her more deeply than anyone else ever had. She told her heart that the pain would ease, should ease, but the wound remained constant and raw. She had heard the old adage of time healing all wounds, but feared whoever made up old adages had a mean sense of humor. She had a measure of peace, but she couldn't find a sense of completeness. A part of her was missing. She found herself wishing for a case of selective amnesia, something to blank out the bittersweet memories of falling in love. Oh, if only she didn't know now what she didn't know then.

The days ceased to have names. One afternoon—it might have been Friday or Monday or Thursday—she decided to set up an old easel and paint set left behind by the houseboat's former owner. She had never tried her hand at painting, but it was a beautiful day, and she was in the mood to be creative. In lieu of a painter's smock she wore the brief yellow bikini she had purchased in Laguna, the swimsuit Billy had never seen. Her hair was parted into pigtails, not a stylish look but very good for keeping wind-blown hair away from wet oils. She painted with great enthusiasm, recreating a fat yellow sun over a huge expanse of summer-blue water. The painting needed a focal point, she decided, chewing thoughtfully on the end of her paint brush.

And that was how Billy found her.

She was unaware of his approach, his footsteps on the dock lost in the soft wash of the waves against the boat. He watched her for the longest time, his heart suspended in his chest. She was utterly absorbed in her painting, brows drawn together fiercely. Her pigtails made her look twelve years old, escaped strands flying wildly around her face. Her swimsuit made her look quite a bit older than twelve. In fact, the sight of her generous, deeply bronzed curves barely contained by two wisps of buttery-yellow material almost gave him a heart attack.

It took him several minutes before he regained the power of speech. "Can I come aboard?" He was terrified she would turn him away. He was ecstatic just to see her again. He felt like a confused stranger in Billy Lucas's body.

The woman-child in yellow froze, paintbrush hanging in midair. Then, very slowly, she turned her head to look at Billy. "What…what are you doing here?"

She had paint on her chin and the tip of her nose. Her feet were bare, toes curled tightly around the bottom rung of a wooden deck chair. Billy's heart swelled in his chest with fierce, protective love. The world would never see her like this again.

He stopped praying that he would say the right things. He started praying for the ability to say anything. Finally, in a hoarse, shaky voice, "I came to see if your brother was right."

Amazingly, Julie reached inside herself and found enough composure to turn back to her painting. As she dipped her brush in paint, she asked carelessly, "Right about what?"

"He said when a woman loved a man, she could forgive him."

Julie realized she had just painted a huge pink cloud.

She scooted her chair sideways, to block Billy's view. She savaged herself inside, trying to stem the tide of panic sweeping her from head to foot. Even now she ached for this man who had betrayed her and hurt her more deeply than anyone else ever had. She had told herself she was healing, but the open wound in her heart remained constant and raw. She closed her eyes tightly, grateful her back was to him. "Harris is as innocent as I once was. He probably believes in happy endings, too."

Billy stepped aboard without waiting for her permission. He very much doubted he would get it, anyway. He watched every muscle in her body tense as he walked closer. Taking those few steps, unsure of anything, was the hardest thing he had ever done. Harder than heading into a blind alley after a shooter, harder than being shot himself, harder than facing his own wretched mistakes. He had never felt more vulnerable in his life. Big, strong Billy Lucas, survivor of the dirty city streets, needed a bulletproof vest for his poor heart. What a poet she had turned him into.

"I didn't," he said quietly. "I never believed in happy endings."

"Obviously," Julie snapped, unable to keep the bitterness from her voice. "And you turned me into a cynic as well." She couldn't just sit there with him so close, especially when she was all but naked. It was as though they had never been together before, and all her old walls were up. She turned her painting over, put her brush down on the table and stood up, wrapping her arms self-consciously around her chest. "I'm cold. I'm going below to put something on."

"Julie, please—"

"I'll be back," she said shortly, turning away so he couldn't see the panic in her eyes.

"I'll wait."

"Whatever."

Below deck, Julie leaned against the closet door and concentrated on breathing. She had forgotten the sheer physical impact he had on her. His hair had been cut, which was surprising, but he still wore it fairly long, carelessly brushed back from his face and ears. His jeans fit as beautifully as ever, giving wonderful definition to his male body. His lightweight white cotton shirt was rolled up casually at the cuffs, emphasizing the muscles in his powerful brown arms.

He was quite beautiful. Even liars could be quite beautiful.

She had no idea why he had come to her after three long weeks. In the back of her mind she had almost expected him at first. But as the days wore on, she stopped hoping against hope to see him on deck in the morning when she first came upstairs, his wide shoulders outlined against the blazing Florida sky. And now, when she had finally accepted the fact that he hadn't cared enough to even try and see her, he showed up out of the blue. And not only that, but he showed up talking about happy endings. How *dare* he?

When she went back on deck, she wore a simple, pinstriped sundress with a deep scoop neck. The paint on her nose and chin had been washed off, the pigtails were gone and her composure was back in place. She padded over to the table, starting to clear up her paints. Billy watched her, leaning against the railing with his thumbs hooked in the pockets of his jeans. His heart was stuck painfully in his dry throat.

"You were saying?" she asked coldly.

Billy swallowed hard. She wasn't making this easy, but then, he hadn't expected it to be easy. "I was saying I never believed in happy endings...until I met you. I had no reason to. My childhood, my job, my entire life taught me there was no such thing as a happy ending. I expected the worst and I got it. Hell, that attitude kept me alive. That's why...when I met you, I wasn't prepared. It never occurred to me I had a chance at anything or anyone like you.''

"You don't," Julie said flatly. "Love involves a certain amount of trust, don't you think? I could never be with someone I don't trust. Not to mention the fact you didn't care enough to fight for me. How long has it been since I left California? Almost a *month*. Whatever possessed you to come looking for me now? Don't tell me a nifty detective like yourself couldn't track me down.''

Billy dropped his head back on his neck, staring at the sky till he saw nothing but exploding sunspots. "Julie... I've known where you were almost since the day you left. Harris told me.''

"You called him?" Julie asked, almost inaudibly.

"No." This wasn't going to reflect well on him, Billy realized. Julie didn't understand his absence had been a form of well deserved self-punishment. "He flew out to California and we had a talk. He gave me your address. Unfortunately, I thought—I guess I still think—that you deserve far better than an ex-undercover cop whose only redeeming quality is staying alive.''

Julie closed her eyes briefly. When she opened them again, there was no hint of emotion in her expression. "Well, if that's what you believe, you must be right. I do deserve better than what you were willing to give me. I want you to leave, Billy.''

He started toward her. "Julie—"

"No!" She thrust out her hand, planting it hard on his chest. "Don't you dare come a step closer. You are...you are…'' She didn't have a lot of experience with swear-words, and nothing suitably insulting was coming to her. Finally she settled for a three-letter word instead of four. ''You're *bad,* and I'll never let you hurt me again! I gave you everything, and you couldn't even give me the truth. You couldn't handle a happy ending, Billy. It would ruin your concept of a cold and hopeless world. You'd have to believe in something and someone, and that's just too much trouble for a disillusioned guy like you. This way, you never have to stick your neck out. At least, not emotionally.''

''Julie, I was wrong. I've learned that in the past few weeks. I need hope and love as much as anyone else. I need you. Heaven knows you could do better, but I love you.''

''That's the first time you've ever said that to me,'' Julie said dully. ''I'm just sorry it's too late.''

Billy stared at her long and hard. He had never begged for anything in his life. He had taken things, found things, forced things, but never had he begged. His pride was in shreds; he would go down on his knees gladly, but the look in her eyes was unmistakable. *Too little, too late.*

He memorized her one last time. Childlike sun-colored hair, the simple cotton dress, the sunburned skin peeling on her small shoulders. Her eyes so big and dark they seemed to eat up her beautiful face. He'd put that pain in those eyes. Her disillusionment had been a gift from the master. ''I'm so sorry,'' he said, straight from his heart. Just like his mother had said to him, trying to apologize for things she could never change. ''I'm so very sorry, sweet girl.''

And he turned and walked away.

Julie stared at his back, absolutely dumbfounded. ''How dare you walk away like that!''

Billy stopped short, looking at her over his shoulder. "What?"

"Haven't you learned *anything*?" Julie was just a half step away from a full-blown and well-earned temper tantrum. Hysteria was also creeping up on her, judging by the hectic rhythm of her pulse. "Don't you have any idea what you have put me through? I have been suffering, I have been aching, I have been missing you like hell and you just *give up*?"

Billy turned slowly, his jaw hanging. The tiniest seed of hope whispered to life within his heart. "You told me to give up."

"Do you do everything you're told? Don't you have a mind of your own? Aren't you familiar with the concept of fighting for anything besides your own skin? Or am I not worth fighting for? What we had was real, even if your story wasn't."

"What are you saying?" Billy whispered, afraid to hope.

"I don't know what I'm saying! I'm mad at you. You say you love me, but it didn't stop you from hurting me."

"Of course it didn't," Billy said softly. "Just because you love someone doesn't mean you'll never do something that might hurt them. It goes along with the risk you take."

"Well, you're not willing to take much of a risk if you're already on your way home. What about hope, Billy? What about dreams? What about persistence?"

"I think I'm losing my mind," Billy muttered, only half kidding. A new light came into his eyes, a light of cautious hope. He took one step toward her, and she didn't jump over the side, which he considered a good sign. He took another. "Julie? Are you giving me a second chance?"

"I'm not giving you anything," she retorted. "You'll have to work for it. Long and hard, because I'm worth it! Damn it, I'm the most wonderful thing that's ever happened to you, and it's high time you realized it. Just once in your life believe in something!"

She was getting herself all worked up, and Billy knew of only one way to stop the poor child from hyperventilating. He put his hands on her arms, jerking her none-too-gently towards him. His mouth swooped over hers, cutting short her tirade very effectively. He kissed her long and hard, as instructed, his mouth slanting sideways in desperate hunger. Tongues danced, hot and welcoming, while their bodies fused with instant heat. Billy's blood was on fire, wanting this woman, this chance, more than anything he had ever wanted in his life. He was afraid of allowing himself to believe in a miracle like Julie Roper, but it didn't frighten him half as much as the idea of living without her.

When they broke from the kiss, Julie was crying. But she was hanging on to him with a death grip at the same time, so Billy allowed himself to hope the tears were happy tears.

"Why did it take you so long?" she asked, hope, anger and love washing through her like a tide. "I waited and waited…but you never came after me."

"I was being upstanding," Billy explained, wiping away her tears with shaking fingers. "Because I wasn't worthy of you. Because I had hurt you so deeply, I needed to inflict the same pain on myself. Then I finally realized that being upstanding stinks."

"I waited so long," she said again, letting go of him long enough to slash at the tears on her cheeks. "I was afraid I wasn't worth fighting for. I kept telling myself

you would find me, but the days came and went, and...
Billy, I've never hurt like that.''

"I'm so sorry," he said, his heart aching in his chest.
"You are worth fighting for, Julie. You're worth living
and dying for. I'm the one who didn't feel worthy. I've
always been separate from the rest of the world. For whatever twisted reason, I'd always found comfort in the fact
I didn't need anyone. I thought I lived every crazy day to
the fullest, but I was wrong. I know now I never stopped
long enough to let my heart breathe, to let any kind of
hope to grow inside me.''

Julie placed trembling palms on either side of his
cheeks. "Did you think I was any different? Harris was
always telling me I had 'everything.' I couldn't figure out
what it was I was missing. Then I met you, and I had my
answer. *You* were missing.''

"Give me another chance," Billy said quietly, seeing
her through suddenly misty eyes. "Give me just one more
shot at happiness. I swear you'll never be sorry.''

Words failed her, but she managed a shaky kiss on his
lips. The shaky kiss turned into a confident kiss, and confidence burned into passion. They were suddenly gasping,
twisting their bodies to find ways to be closer. The sun
rained down on them, heating their skin. This sensual fire
was a healing balm for two bruised hearts.

"It's not just this, Julie," Billy managed between gasping breaths. "It's so much more than physical love. You
have to believe—''

"Be quiet Billy," said the not-so-innocent blond
woman-child in a throaty, sensually charged voice. "I
know what this is. The passion, the pleasure, the
pain...it's all a part of love. I learned that from you. And
right now I need...''

"Right now?" Billy asked, a familiar, love-hazed smile

glinting in his blue, blue eyes. "What do you need right now, angel girl?"

"Come with me," she whispered confidentially, taking his hand. She led him down a narrow flight of stairs that descended into cool shadows, happily instructing him to mind his head on the low ceiling. He did as he was told, like a good boy. She stopped at the doorway of her living quarters, looking at him expectantly.

"What?" Billy asked.

"There's a wonderful tradition of men carrying women over a threshold to begin a new adventure together." She batted her long lashes at him. "Please?"

Again he did as he was told like a good boy. And then he laid her gently on her low bed and stopped acting like a good boy. He had known from the beginning that Julie was a woman who wanted to experience unfamiliar things. He had a few good ideas and did his best to gratify her wishes and dreams.

The sundress had billowed up above her knees when he'd laid her on the mattress. He encouraged the northbound direction, slipping his hands over her silky thighs and pushing the soft cotton even higher. He started at her ankles, kissing the exact spot where her pulse thundered and skipped. His fingers wove intricate patterns on her skin as his mouth traveled upwards, kissing her knees, her thighs, leaving a trail of tingling fire in his wake.

Julie was gasping almost from the beginning, her hands tangled in his thick, cool hair for some kind of balance that didn't come. She was tipping and swirling, riding a wave of delight and desire that eclipsed anything that had come before. She had no self-control and no desire to find any. She was simply flesh and blood, hypnotized by his sensual, clever hands and knowing mouth. He knew secrets she didn't. He probably had a whole closet of them, enough to fuel the fire for a lifetime.

And she wanted to know them all.

"Billy?" she breathed. "Do something for me, please…"

He raised up on his elbows and stared down at this amazing creation of his desire. Julie's glistening hair was spread across the pristine white pillow like a golden wedding veil. Her parted lips were damp, the color in her face hectic. One strap of her sundress had slipped over her shoulder, exposing the upper curve of her breast. "Absolutely. Positively. Anything."

Still gasping, she gave him an adorable, lopsided smile and ruffled his tangled hair. "Such enthusiasm. You don't need to be careful with me, you know. When we were in California, I know you were…cautious. You can let go, now. You don't need to protect me like that. I don't *want* you to protect me like that."

He gave her his old familiar smile, cocky and just dangerous enough to be irresistible. "So, what you're saying…?"

"You know exactly what I'm saying." And with that, she grabbed his shoulders and pulled him down to her, kissing him with all the passion and fever trembling in her body. Her mouth opened and her tongue danced, hungry and wild. Billy was stunned for a moment, unable to believe this was the cool porcelain princess he had once been hired to protect. Then, mindful of her instructions, he "let go."

He rolled over on the bed, keeping Julie's body fused against his. He was the teacher now, and he intended to make her deeply aware of the fact. And the teacher began at the beginning. "Have you ever made out?" he murmured against her parted mouth. "Really made out?"

Julie's eyes widened then closed as he gently kissed each hypersensitive lid. "Before you, I never did much of...oooh, that feels good..."

He pressed a smile against the pulse at the base of her throat beating like a trip-hammer. "You smell wonderful, like sunshine and flowers...."

He abandoned conversation, sliding his lips from her throat to her ear, delicately touching the soft folds. Ankles, throat, ears...all the places Julie would have never considered erogenous zones. He held her beautiful face between his hands as he returned to her mouth. He kissed her with the brief tickle of butterfly wings, he kissed her hard, he kissed her deeply and thoroughly. Julie couldn't get enough of him, the wet silk of his lips, his skin, his tongue hungry on her mouth. Through the gauzy screen of growing passion she became conscious of his hands. He had pushed aside the remaining strap of her dress, exposing her heated skin almost to her waist. Immediately she wanted his hands and mouth *there,* but he seemed determined to avoid the sweet heaviness of her breasts. He trailed the tip of his tongue across the delicate skin of her collarbone, then pressed his mouth directly over her pulse. He suckled gently there, making Julie gasp and clench his shoulders with white-knuckled hands. Each touch set her nerve endings on fire, making her skin dance with tingling nerves. And technically, he hadn't really done *anything* yet. Heaven help her....

Billy was suffering his own burning hunger, and deliberately heightened the sensation by pressing his hips against hers, pushing and rocking in a sexual pantomime. At the same time, he finally let his hands cup the full weight of her breasts, kneading slowly, lifting, drawing a circle of her nipples with his finger. Julie groaned with pleasure-pain, her head rocking from side to side on the pillow. Her hands were helpless, moving from his hair to his back to his hips, anything that might bring him closer still. Quite deliberately he worked her into a soft frenzy, a moment in time where thought and logic ceased to exist.

Julie gave a soft cry of frustration as his mouth loved her breasts with the same exquisite attention to detail his hands had. With less control his shaky hands pushed her dress higher, then slipped beneath the crumpled cotton. What he felt there made him groan.

"You aren't wearing underwear. There's nothing on under the dress," he said hoarsely. "You're killing me, Julie...."

Julie was so focused on her aching body, she hardly heard his words. He was not inflicting any physical pain whatsoever, yet he constantly heightened the wonderful sensual agony. She wanted this and more, wanted to keep pace with him while he led her through his astonishing sexual playground. They rolled side-to-side on the bed, never pausing in their hungry kisses. Their legs intertwined, hands clutched and hips rocked harder against each other. She loved what she was learning, loved the way her body answered to his. Still, their clothes got in their way....

She amazed herself when she gathered enough willpower to suddenly slip from the bed. Billy nearly beat the pillow senseless with the force of his frustration. "Honey...?"

"Watch," Julie whispered.

She reached behind her back, finding the zipper of her dress. She pulled it down very slowly, though her hands were shaking badly with sexual need. Billy's eyes widened as he realized precisely what she was doing. She held his gaze in the shadows, never blinking, never turning away. Her body began to sway gently from side to side, allowing the soft summer dress to slip to her waist, her hips …and down to the floor, the blue-and-white material billowing around her ankles.

Billy had no words. He had no breath, no control over the sexual chaos her actions inspired. The teacher became the pupil then, fully aware of how much raw hunger her body pulled from deep in his loins. Never breaking contact with her eyes, he rolled off the bed and removed his clothes. They went flying, landing here and there. At that moment he wasn't capable of deliberate concentration.

Julie knelt down on her side of the bed, her index finger crooking with sweet insistence. ''Come here, Billy Lucas.'' Then, with a trembling smile, ''Please.''

At that point, Billy surrendered.

He was down on the bed beside her with a sharp, indrawn breath, anxious and desperate to feel her body against his. His hands were everywhere, his lips trailing kisses on her bare skin. He needed, he wanted, he loved. Never in his life had he known a hunger like this. He rolled Julie onto her back, their legs tangled. Her hands clutched fistfuls of the crumpled white bedsheet at either side of her hips. She gave herself up to loving, letting her last few coherent thoughts drift into the shadowy corners of the small, quiet cabin. She felt his awe of her natural sexuality and reveled in it. She wanted to be his equal in every way, wanted to please him and entice him even further. She basked in her power as a woman, a power that would have been sadly lacking had he been anything but her first—and last—true love. She gave herself with fierce abandon, reveling in the growing intensity between their hot bodies. They were perfectly matched in desire and emotion. They communicated perfectly, knowing precisely what the other needed, because they each needed it. Their bodies were damp and straining as they climbed closer to a blazing glimpse of eternity. They ceased to have identities beyond love and lover. Whenever Julie raised her lids and gazed into his fever-bright eyes, he felt as if she were taking off all her clothes again. He was astounded and fiercely grateful that she felt enough security in his love to abandon all caution. And somehow he knew it would always be this way between them, each forever finding a home in the other.

When he finally entered her, Julie was mindless and shivering. Her fists pounded the mattress softly, her head thrown back with passion. It had never been like this before. Billy's strong protective instincts had kept a subconscious rein on his passions. Now, knowing she wanted and needed this as badly as he did, he finally let go of the last shreds of his control. His breath, like hers, came fast and deep, as if they had been running hard. Julie's hands clung helplessly to the smooth skin of his shoulders, fingers splayed over the erotic tension in his muscles. Ever so slowly he pressed deeper into her body, and deeper still. She writhed and groaned, trying desperately to get close enough. Somehow she knew this ecstasy was rare, that only those who truly loved could achieve such a perfect union. For a brief moment, she felt sorry for all the couples in the world who casually practiced the act of loving without *feeling* love for their partner. They hadn't a clue what they were losing.

Her eyes misted up as his body rhythm became sharper, harder, more possessive. This was the final dance, being lifted again and again to dizzying heights. They gasped together, rocked together, pushed together, until they found the ultimate experience…that few seconds of anguished delight as they reached the highest plateau of physical demands. She saw him like a dream above her, loving the passion in his eyes, the damp smoothness of his skin, the weight of his body filling, completing and possessing her. White-hot rapture swirled into her senses, growing like a whirlwind. Still she held his eyes, watching him find the same burning enchantment almost simultaneously. His muscles grew taut, his breathing ceased and his body shuddered with the force of his release. Beneath him, Julie gasped and cried with a sweet delirium, tears spilling over her cheeks. This was life, this was rapture, this was the wistful dream and fantasy of every man and woman alive.

This was love.

Later, he moistened a soft cloth and wiped away the tracks of her tears. He had to continually touch her, clinging to her like a lifeline. He knew how fortunate they were, two people who had come so close to losing the most important gift either had ever been given. He was greatly humbled, so thankful that true love was capable of surviving the mistakes of foolish mortals. It had been much too close a call, and they shook with the force of their relief and joy. What fate had denied Billy for so long was finally granted. He had something and someone to believe in and belong to, a love that promised a lifetime of bright tomorrows.

"Would you really have left me today?" Julie whispered as they lay side by side, face-to-face. "After all we've been through...would you really have walked away so easily?"

Billy lovingly smoothed her tangled hair away from her face. "No, little love. I would have talked myself into coming back tomorrow, and the day after that and the day after that. Love is worth fighting for, and it's worth hurting for. You taught me that. Heaven knows you could do better than a reformed cynic without a drop of blue blood, but you would never find anyone who loves you like I do. If you'll just believe in me one more time, I swear I'll give you the world.

"You already have," Julie sighed, a goofy smile completing her lovestruck expression. She kissed Billy on the chin, then rubbed his nose with hers. "So, do you like your new home?"

"I love it. You're here, aren't you? Still…why did you choose a houseboat?"

"I'll let you in on a secret," Julie whispered confidentially. "You can't have security gates on a houseboat."

He shivered as she kissed his neck with a soft, lingering sensuality. "No security gates?"

"No fences, no gates, no walls. Just you and me against the world, Officer. What do you think about that?"

Billy smiled, folding her up in his arms as tenderly and carefully as he would a delicate flower. Still, he knew only too well she was anything but fragile. This amazing woman—his amazing woman—was far stronger than she looked.

"I think the world had better watch out," he said.

*   *   *   *   *

Silhouette® *Desire*

invites you to enter the
exclusive, masculine world of the...

TEXAS Cattleman's Club

Lone Star Jewels

Silhouette Desire's powerful miniseries features five wealthy Texas bachelors—all members of the state's most prestigious club—who set out to recover the town's jewels...and discover their true loves!

MILLIONAIRE M.D.—January 2001
by Jennifer Greene (SD #1340)

WORLD'S MOST ELIGIBLE TEXAN—February 2001
by Sara Orwig (SD #1346)

LONE STAR KNIGHT—March 2001
by Cindy Gerard (SD #1353)

HER ARDENT SHEIKH—April 2001
by Kristi Gold (SD #1358)

TYCOON WARRIOR—May 2001
by Sheri WhiteFeather (SD #1364)

Available at your favorite retail outlet.

Silhouette®
Where love comes alive™

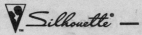

Desire

January 2001
TALL, DARK & WESTERN
#1339 by Anne Marie Winston

February 2001
THE WAY TO A RANCHER'S HEART
#1345 by Peggy Moreland

March 2001
MILLIONAIRE HUSBAND
#1352 by Leanne Banks
Million-Dollar Men

April 2001
GABRIEL'S GIFT
#1357 by Cait London
Freedom Valley

May 2001
THE TEMPTATION OF
RORY MONAHAN
#1363 by Elizabeth Bevarly

June 2001
A LADY FOR LINCOLN CADE
#1369 by BJ James
Men of Belle Terre

MAN OF THE MONTH

For twenty years Silhouette has been giving
you the ultimate in romantic reads. Come join
the celebration as some of your favorite authors
help celebrate our anniversary with the most
sensual, emotional love stories ever!

Available at your favorite retail outlet.

Silhouette®
Where love comes alive™

Visit Silhouette at www.eHarlequin.com   SDMOM01